SNOW ON MAGNOLIAS

by Hattie Mae

Books in the Bon Amie series

Welcome
To Bon Amie
Hattie Mae

Dedication

When I was growing up in Louisiana, I loved hearing all the old sayings handed down from generation. One of my dad's favorites was, "you can always tell a true Cajun when they can look at a field of rice and tell you how much gravy it would take."

So I dedicate this book to all the hard-working rice farmers out there. It goes great with my gravy.

I would also like to dedicate this book to my dear husband, Ernest, who has read my books and never misses a chance to brag about them to whomever will listen.

And also my three children and their spouses and six grandchildren who make me proud everyday. You are my blessings in action.

Chapter One

Sam LeBlanc sat in the old rocker; it's paint worn from daily use. He rocked gently in the familiar chair on the gallery outside his bedroom.

The smell of fresh rain lingered in the air; a ring around the moon gave promise of more to come. Was there anywhere on earth that smelled as great after a rain than Louisiana? He thought not. But along with the cooling rain came the heavy thick humidity. What did his mom say? Something about with every cup of good there's a spoonful of bad. His feet rested on the banister as he swatted a mosquito whining around his ear.

His T-shirt clung to his body, cooled by a light breeze rustling through the mighty oaks. Oaks his ancestors had planted and made sure would withstand time. His family had held this land for generations, and with his help he expected it to be held for generations to come. Sam could imagine the hands of his kin reaching across the past to lend help when he was in need. He knew it deep in his soul and felt their presence as they watched over the plantation and the family it housed.

He released a heavy sigh. Harvest time was approaching and he had yet to find the help needed to cut the rice, and now, with Odelia's broken arm, he would have to find someone to assist her.

As he listened to the rain frogs, his body relaxed. Late night, his favorite time, with everyone asleep and worries laid aside, all seemed right with the world. He knew he worried too much and should give credit to his brothers, but he just couldn't let go of being in charge.

He stifled a yawn, and stretched out his arms. The sight of headlights as they snaked down the winding lane caught his eye. He leaned against the banister. Who could be calling at this hour, this far off the main road? Someone with bad news or someone up to no good.

Just last year, he would have hoped it was Lisa. But not now. His love for her died during the nights he'd held his daughters as they cried for her return. And the days when he comforted them and assured them they were not to blame. Never again would he allow a woman to enter their lives and cause them pain.

The car made a sharp right turn away from the main road, stopping at the small house where Odelia lived. She was so much more than a caregiver for his family. She'd come to them just before his mom had died and been more of a second mother to he and his brothers. Sam walked down the stairs and strolled across the covered walk leading to that side of his home. In the shadows of one of the oak trees, he picked up a large branch off the ground to serve as a weapon, just in case, moved a clump of Spanish moss out of his way, and waited.

Lights from the side of the house illuminated the area. The car stopped. The driver's door opened and bare legs unfolded out of the small car. The legs of a woman.

Sam dropped the branch and stood ready to confront the trespasser when the rest of her body followed the legs out of the car.

He stared in disbelief as the redhead stood in the beam of the floodlights with hands on her hips and stared at the charred part of Odelia's house. The smell of smoke from the fire that happened two weeks ago still clung to the thick air.

He looked at his watch. 1:16 in the morning. A redheaded woman.

Everyone in Louisiana knew what that meant, especially Sam, and there she stood.

"Damn," Sam said under his breath. His brothers would say he only had one oar in the water, just his luck. His superstitions all had an ounce of truth in them, and this one was no exception. A red-headed woman on his property on a Monday, he now knew his week was doomed.

I don't need this now. He'd enough trouble finding workers to bring in the rice crop. And being able to keep his brothers motivated to work the fields was another nest of trouble. Nothing he did came easy now days, nothing at all. No, he didn't need any bad luck this week. And he certainly didn't need it coming from a woman. But there stood trouble right before his eyes, shapely legs and all.

He stepped out of the shadows into the light. "May I help you?" he asked.

"Mercy!" She spun around, her eyes wide with fear.

"Ma'am are you lost?" Sam watched as her eyes turned to liquid and her chin began to quiver.

Sam dug his shoe into the soft dirt. Aw hell. This was not going well.

"Look lady, if you're in trouble or something?"

She stiffened her back and made a quick swipe with the back of her hand across her eyes. "No. I'm not in trouble, I'm here to see my Aunt Odelia. Does she still live here?" Her voice shook as she turned back towards the damaged house. "Is she all right?"

A lost memory tugged at his brain. His steps took him closer for him to study her features. A smile drifted across his lips. "Well, well, I remember you. You're that girl that spent the summer with Odelia. You're little Rose. All grown up."

Remembering her shapely legs when they glided out of the car, he now took in the rest of her. Her arms wrapped around her small waist. Her full lips drew his focus to the tiny mole at the right of her top lip. Still there. "I remember you all right. You stayed in my pocket that whole summer. You were afraid of everything but brave enough not to show it."

Beads of sweat popped up on Sam's forehead. His throat tightened, he remembered something else, Rose was the first girl he'd ever kissed. How old had he been, twelve, maybe thirteen? He'd kissed many girls, but he couldn't think of when.

Thunder rolled in the distance. The humidity wasn't the only thing heavy in the air tonight. Trouble was brewing and it was coming fast.

Rose shifted her weight, her voice low and husky.
"You have a good memory. I remember that summer too. It seems like there were two or three rowdy boys that summer. Which one are you?"
His voice got hung in the back of his throat so he coughed. He was not a young boy with first kisses on his mind but a grown man with good southern manners.

"I'm Sam. Forgive my lack of hospitality, Rose. You must be dead on your feet. Odelia has long been in bed. She's staying in the main house while her place is rebuilt. She had a kitchen fire a couple of weeks ago."

He tugged on his ear and continued. Why was he so nervous, it had to be the red hair? "I'll get your bag and show you to one of the bedrooms."

Sam lifted a large suitcase out of her backseat and placed it on the ground. He glanced back inside the car to see if there was another bag. Yellow

Post-its hung on the dashboard, and candy wrappers littered the floor. Several other bags and boxes were crammed inside the car. *How long was she staying?*

"Leave your car. Someone will bring it around in the morning. Your things will be safe." Sam bent over to pick up the bag at the same time as Rose. Her hair brushed his face. Soft as a kitten's belly. He inhaled – fresh peaches warmed by the sun. He coughed again, to clear his head.

He walked up the path. "Did you get lost? Is that why you're so late?" he asked.

"No, I planned to start out sooner, but I kept finding one more thing to do. I'm inclined to do that. Some people might think I'm flighty." Tucking a stray curl behind her ear, she added, "I like to consider myself a multi-tasker. I do agree that sometimes, like today, I underestimate my time." She shifted her purse to the other shoulder. "I certainly didn't mean to arrive at someone's home this late, but I never saw one motel, not one that I would stay in, since I left New Orleans. I apologize."

Sam guessed Rose's height to be only about five feet, so he slowed his gait, but she kept up with the stride of his six foot two frame. And kept on talking. For a little woman, she sure could talk.

"Odelia didn't say anything at dinner about you coming tonight. You know she talks about you all the time, I can't believe she didn't yell it from the rafters."

"Oh, I didn't tell her. I meant to. But things happened and I thought--- well never mind what I thought. I should have called," she said.

Opening the front door, he lowered his voice. "No need to get the whole house up. We've got a busy day tomorrow." He led her up the large staircase, softly lit from sconces on the wall. The steps, covered with carpet in shades of pinks and grays, showed wear from the years of use, and they creaked ever so lightly as they walked. At the top of the stairs, he opened a door on his right and flipped on the light.

"I trust this will do." He gestured his hand to encompass the whole room. A large grin spread across his face and pride lit his eyes.

"Yes. The room is lovely, thank you," she said.

Sam was proud of his home. He knew he was fortunate to have inherited this grand plantation. Sam wished all his brothers held the same love for *Annees Passees*. The name on the Plantation, which meant 'years gone by,' fit it perfectly and had also been passed on including the rest of the housing and land.

"Sam, don't tell Aunt Odelia I'm here. I have a habit of getting up early so I would like to surprise her," she whispered.

"Okay, I know she will be happy to see you." Sam placed his hand on the doorknob and turned back. "Will your husband be joining you? Odelia told us you were getting married last month."

"No, I didn't get married. In fact don't ever plan to." Rose eased the door shut, forcing Sam to back out of the room into the hall. "Ever." The door closed except for a crack that Rose peaked at Sam through. "Goodnight, Sam, and thanks."

If she had to talk about that humiliating day when Ted deserted her at the altar one more time, she thought she would fade away. That was the main reason she was here. To forget about him and to not see the disapproving look in her mother's eyes. Of course the plea from her Aunt that she needed help made it an easy decision to jump in the car and drive away from Atlanta. It was time for her to rely on herself.

She ran her fingers over the smooth wood of several antique pieces of furniture placed around the large room. A room that calmed her, inspired her. This was a writer's room if ever she'd seen one. Maybe she'd come to the right place to renew herself after all.

A green satin lined full-tester bed dominated the room. Colors of soft greens and mauves graced the walls and drapes, offering a hint of peace and acceptance. A hand-stitched Ohio star quilt made of the same mauves and greens, a slight shade darker, covered the bed. A pillow scarf framed by a tiny row of tatted lace with tiny roses completed the edging as it concealed the feather pillows.

French doors that led to the gallery spanning the second floor caught her attention. A full moon flooded the area as lighting danced in the distance. Large white rockers with blue checked cushions lined the wall. A porch swing creaked as it moved lightly in welcome at one end. Other French doors opened onto the gallery and Rose wondered whose rooms they harbored.

This place was more beautiful than she remembered. The large white columns connected both floors like a gentle giant holding this home steadfast. Was Sam the gentle giant keeping watch over his family? Why else would he have been up at this hour?

She had come back to this place hoping to find---what? Something made her feel welcome that summer she visited. She remembered feeling safe. Peaceful even.

A perfect place to find me again, this might be my last chance to find the real Rose. Not the Rose, Mother tried to mold and still found fault with. *No more Mother, no more picking a man of certain standards, and then hating me when I can't hold on to them, no more wanting me to be someone I'm not.*

Rose washed her face, threw on a T-shirt, and crawled under the quilt. The feather mattress engulfed her in its folds, holding her close keeping her safe. Her eyes were heavy as she thought of her meeting with Sam.

Yes Sam, this room will suit me fine. She turned over and plumped her pillow. *I remember you too. I also remember a kiss.* What girl ever forgot her first kiss? Rose ran her finger over her lips and smiled.

They'd been trying to catch bullfrogs along the canal bank and stopped to rest. Sam reached over and wiped perspiration off the top of her lip. Then he smiled a slow crooked grin and kissed her ever so lightly full on the lips. It was like he sucked the breath right out of her. To hide his embarrassment, he had punched her on the arm and ran off. The rest of the summer she caught him watching her, especially her mouth. Had he felt the flutter in his stomach like she had? Surprised that after all this time she'd never forgotten that kiss. She turned over in bed again and closed her eyes.

Rose shifted her weight and felt her body sink a little deeper into the mattress. Sun from a nearby window warmed her face as a fresh smell of clean starched linens caressed her nose. She blinked her eyes a couple of times before slowly opening them, focusing on the vision before her. She slowly closed her lids again. Only to jerk them open and let out a piercing scream.

"Gracious, merciful me!"

There staring back were her own eyes. Frightening eyes reflected in a mirror held close to her face by a small giggling girl.

"What in the world do you think you're doing? You nearly scared the life out of me."

The small girl's giggle stopped and a frown replaced her smile. She scooted from the side if the bed and ran to the far side of the room.

Rose stood on shaky legs. The little imp cowered in the corner hugging a well-loved rag doll. Rose's anger now turned to guilt. "Look I'm sorry, but you scared the begeebers out of me."

The sound of stampeding buffaloes came up the stairs. Sam and two more men rushed in her bedroom followed by a girl older than the little one clinging to the wall followed.

"What happened?" Sam asked.

The little girl ran and wrapped her small arms around Sam's leg. "I'm sorry Papa. I didn't know she was the cross kind. I was just trying to see if she was breathing. Really I was."

Sam knelt and gathered the child in his arms. "It's okay, pumpkin." Holding her close he ran his large hands gently over her hair, his voice calm and soothing.

"Lizzy, you know better. Why were you in Miss Rose's room to start with?" he asked his daughter.

"Cuz, when I passed her room I heard a sound. Her door was not locked, so I creped up to her bed, and I couldn't see her moving. She looked like Sleeping Beauty. But she's not. Sleeping Beauty would never yell at me." Lizzy peaked at Rose through her fingers.

"I told her I was sorry," Rose said. A lump in her throat blocked her words as she looked at the three men. All turned their accusing eyes on her.

You messed up again, the voice of her mother echoed in her head.

"I really didn't mean to scare her, but after all, she was... she did..." Rose sighed and bowed her head. "I'm sorry Lizzy."

Sam stood with Lizzy in his arms.

"No harm done." Sam followed his brothers' gaze to Rose. A deep red color moved up his neck into his face. "If my brothers are through gawking at you, we'll leave and give you a chance to put the rest of your clothes on. Meet us downstairs for breakfast. Your aunt will be very happy to see you." Sam offered a tight grin.

He lifted his little girl's face up to his, and a warm loving smile took his firm lips. "Lizzy, tell Miss Rose you're sorry for scaring her."

"I sorry, Miss Rose," Lizzy whispered as she kept her eyes down, avoiding looking at Rose or anywhere in her direction.

"Come along Bea, the excitement's over. Time to eat." Sam put his free arm around the older girl's stiff shoulders, and they all filed out of her room as the older girl shot Rose a cold accusing stare.

The voice of one of the other brothers drifted upstairs.

"What's the world coming to when Sammy Boy invites a red- headed woman into his home on a Monday? You sure are slipping."

Their laughter and teasing continued as they walked down the stairs.

Maybe this was not the place to refill her soul. Sam made her feel like an intruder last night, and from his looks this morning, he still considered her one.

That man had the ability to sear right through her with those eyes. And the uncanny way he held eye contact made her want to confess everything she'd ever done wrong. What color were those eyes anyway? Crap. Shaking her head, she allowed the breath she was holding to escape. "Who cares? I must have been crazy driving up to someone's house at one in the morning unannounced," she mumbled.

Rose squeezed her eyes closed, but could still see what she considered Sam's disapproving look. She had seen that same look in many men's eyes.

No matter. She was starting new. And after all, Aunt Odelia had asked for her help. 'Don't bother the boys about me wanting help,' she'd said. Aunt Odelia didn't want them to know she'd asked for help.

This time would give Rose a chance to set her life straight. She would just have to put up with Sam's looks; anything was better than seeing her picture plastered all over Atlanta and the rumors flying around about her broken engagement.

Throwing on a pair of designer slacks and a matching Gucci blouse, she searched for her shoes, gave up and settled on a pair of slippers. Rose sat at the dresser and tried to smooth her hair. Thank goodness her mother wasn't there to see what the humidity was doing to her natural curls.

Rose could hear her repeating the same old speech over and over again.

Do something with your hair, Rose. It's sticking up everywhere. I swear you can't make a silk purse out of a sow's ear no matter how much you try. You're a lost cause. You'll never have class.

Rose's shoulders dropped in defeat. *My God, Mother, I'm a twenty six year old woman, not a little girl full of fear.*

Standing a bit taller she stared at her image. "Well, Mother, you're not here," she said to the woman in the mirror. Who did she have to impress anyway?

As she closed her suitcase, one of the promotional key rings for her latest book caught her eye. She picked up the clear cylinder. Stars and glitter floated in the liquid; maybe this would make amends to Sam's smallest daughter, and just maybe pave the way to her apology. That thought put a bounce in her step all the way to the dining room.

Voices and laughter rang out well before she reached the bottom of the steps. Family voices. Words spoken between people who knew each other well and were not embarrassed to show their love. She froze outside of the door, her feet glued in place. She didn't belong in there. With a family.

"Who's my visitor, Sam? Stop teasing me and tell me or you get no *La Bouillie*."

Now that was a word she'd not heard in a very long time. Rose could taste the warm custard she'd had for breakfast when she'd last visited. Aunt Odelia use to fix it for her when she was young, but what a strange dish to be tempting an adult man. With the sound of her Aunt's voice, she couldn't hold back any longer. She needed someone's approval. Rose rounded the corner and entered the dining room, bumping into one of the chairs. Everyone turned toward the noise. For the second time that morning, she was the center of attention.

"Rose? Is that you?" Her aunt threw her good arm in the air. "Thank you, dear Lord. I hoped you would come." Odelia cooed as she pulled Rose into her ample embrace. "Child, I have waited for this day too long. Every time we've talked on the phone, I'd hoped you meant it when you said you'd see me soon. Now you're here." Odelia moved the loose curl out of Rose's face. "I thought after what that horrible Ted did to you, leaving you at the altar like that, you would find your way back to us." She gave Rose another tight hug. "I was right."

To be held by someone that cared made Rose's insides turn to mush. She swallowed hard trying to keep the tears in control. No way was she going to cry in front of all those men. Especially now that they all knew she'd been left at the altar. Great, now they thought she was not only rude to children but also a big loser who couldn't even hold on to her man. Maybe they were right.

"It's so good to see you, Aunt Odelia." Holding back her feelings just as her mother had taught her, Rose twisted her hands and offered a small smile.

"How about breakfast? I bet you're starving. You need some meat on those poor little bones. What would you like?" Odelia asked fluttering toward the sideboard.

"Sit down, I'll fix my plate." Rose gave her aunt's hand a squeeze, and glanced at the sideboard laden with food. "My goodness are you expecting more people? Look at this spread." Rose could feel the looks on her back before she turned. Everyone was still frozen in place staring at her.

"Eat. Please. I promise not to scream at anyone else this morning. I will watch my manners and only say nice things, so please, eat your breakfast." Rose picked up her plate of food and tried to calm her shaking insides. Utensils scraped against plates and the conversation started again.

Aunt Odelia made room for Rose between her and Sam. His eyes ever watchful as she ate and talked with her beloved aunt.

"May I be excused, Papa? I ate all my eggs," Lizzy said.

"Drink your milk first and stay close to the house, and someone will bring you to Bon Amie to see Trudy."

Rose reached in her pocket and took out the key chain. "Lizzy, before you go outside, I have a little something for you. It's not much but maybe you'll enjoy looking at the stars."

She held it out to the dubious little girl, dark ringlets fell around her beautiful face. Her brown round eyes held such uncertainty and sadness for such a young child. A feeling Rose knew something about, much like her own childhood.

Lizzy took the key chain turned it up and watched the purple stars and glitter slowly move to one end, and then tilted it back and watched them slide the other direction. "Wow. How did you get the stars in here? What does the writing say Papa?" she asked as she shoved it into Sam's hand.

"Let's see, pumpkin, it reads *Look For The Stars* by Dusty Rose.'" He raised his left eyebrow as he looked at Rose. "Is that you?"

"Yes. Dusty Rose is my pen name. *Look For The Stars* was the title of my last book."

Sam stilled one of his brothers' snickers with a stern look.

"What do you say, Lizzy?" Sam reminded her.

"Thank you, Miss Rose."

Rose's heart warmed at the soft words from Lizzy. She turned toward the older girl who sat glaring at her under thick brows. Her blue eyes held a coldness that only a child that had lost her trust could have. She didn't speak, just continued to glare.

"I have another key chain if you would like. Come to my room after breakfast, and I'll get it out for you."

Bea never took her brooding eyes off Rose when she stood. Bea's back was stiff and she folded her arms across her chest. Rose's throat tightened as she remembered she had tried to protect her heart in much the same way as this child, and still caught herself with her arms folded across her heart many times.

"I'm too old for toys," Bea said.

Rose had been dismissed with no uncertainly.

Bea left the table, Lizzy running after her, but she returned to the table for her doll. "Wait, Bea, wait for me and Miss Abby. Don't go so fast."

Something had caused both of these girls hurt. Someone had betrayed them, more than once. Their mother was nowhere in sight, maybe she had something to do with their behavior.

"Bea takes a little time to get to know people. She's kind of a loner," said Aunt Odelia.

"You sure have beautiful red hair," one of Sam's brothers said with a grin on his face. Laughter broke out from the other brother.

Rose put her fork down and turned her attention to the men. "Would someone please tell me why everyone is so worked up over my red hair?"

Sam's brothers both started to talk at the same time.

"Go ahead, Preston. You're about to burst, tell her," Odelia said.

"There's a superstition in Louisiana that if you invite a red-headed woman to your house on a Monday, you'll have bad luck all that week. And our Sammy Boy, here, is a firm believer in superstitions, all superstitions. So needless to say he is waiting for the sky to fall."

"You're crazy, Preston, I'm not superstitious. Just watchful that's all."

"Right, we all know better," Preston said as they continued to razz their brother. But Sam sported a large grin; he seemed to be enjoying the teasing.

The man on Sam's right clanked his fork against his plate.

"Enough of our family's strange personalities, please tell us something about yourself, Rose."

"Lewis I believe you enjoy hearing about people's lives as much as any woman," Sam teased.

Was this the brother in charge, or did that job fall to Sam? Lewis must be the oldest brother according to the dusting of gray at his temples.

"Damn right." Preston dropped his fork on his plate.

"Watch your mouth—" Sam started to correct, but was interrupted.

"I'll be happy to share bits of my life at another time. But I have a few questions." Rose said to the men that sat around the table.

"Could anyone tell me where the magnolia tree is that I kept smelling last night? I searched for one out of my windows and walked out to the gallery, but didn't see any. The smell was so strong it must be close."

Rose glanced into faces lit with smiles around the table.

"That would be *Tante* Ina, our friendly ghost," Preston answered. If one of the brothers were a bigger tease, it would be Preston. He was larger than Sam and Lewis in both height and weight, with dark brown eyes and hair the color of rich chocolate. A tan rugged face with crinkles of laugh lines around his mouth and eyes showed his playfulness and kindness.

Rose returned their smiles. "You're pulling my leg."

"No, he's not. Preston is telling the truth. *Tante* Ina has been with us for as long as stories have been told. She's harmless, just checking you out like she does all of our guests. You'll know soon enough if she accepts you," Sam replied.

"Aunt Odelia, they're teasing me, right?"

"No, honey. What they say is true. But don't let her frighten you. She really is harmless. Besides what true Plantation Home wouldn't have a ghost in residence?"

"If you are afraid, maybe we could pull a bed into your Aunt's room," Sam teased.

Rose raised her nose a little higher in the air. "Don't be ridiculous. I'm not afraid. And besides, I don't believe in ghosts." Even if she were a little afraid, she would never show it. She never had before.

"Of course you're not." Sam turned his attention to his brothers. "If you old hens are through cackling, we have a lot of work to do today. Preston, you said the number two combine was acting up yesterday; we better see what's wrong with that sucker. And we still need to double check the rice bins," Sam said. He turned his attention to Odelia. "Tell Trudy I'll settle up with her later this week. And don't let Bea talk her into a buzz."

Rose smiled. No doubt, Sam was the one in charge.

Preston picked up his hat walked around the table and kissed Odelia on her cheek. "See you later, my queen." Rose stood to help clear the table when Preston scooped her up in his ample arms and gave her a tight hug and kissed her on her cheek. "So glad you came to see us, little Rose. It's nice having a young woman in the house again."

"Put her down, Preston. You need to stop picking up every woman you meet, just because you can." Sam said. "Besides, you better save your hugs for that woman you've been eyeing in Bon Amie. You have yet to share information about who she is or anything about her."

Preston set Rose down gently and winked at her. "I don't know what you're talking about, but I do know, big brother, holding something soft like this might be just what you need." Preston waved his hand and gave Odelia one more pat on her arm. "See you ladies later."

He and Lewis filed out, leaving Sam holding his hat in hand. "Ladies," he muttered and followed.

The house was left with a deafening silence.

"Are they always like that?" Rose asked.

"No, most of the time they're loud and rowdy," Odelia said with a chuckle. A faraway look crossed her face. "But I don't know what I would do without them."

Odelia gave the table one last wipe and pulled out a chair. "Let's sit a spell and I'll tell you what's in store for the next two weeks." Letting out pent up breath, she smiled weakly at Rose. "I'm so sorry, but I think it's more work than I thought it would be for the two of us. I thought I had Mrs. Daigle lined up to help us, but she called to tell me she has the flu. I really planned on her pies for tonight's supper." Odelia rubbed her arm. "Of all times for this old woman to break a bone."

"Aunt Odelia, I'm here and I need this. I can't believe I've never come and helped you before." Rose reached over and took her aunt's hand in hers.

Fighting back the tears, her aunt said, "Don't pay any attention to me Rose, we'll still have time for some long talks. In fact, if you don't mind driving, we can talk in the car. I have to get the girls to town so Trudy can cut their hair. And when we return, I will start my cooking and baking. I won't have a lot of time, but it'll get done. Always does."

Rose followed her aunt to the kitchen. "Even if I'm not much of a cook, I can chop and stir. I could also take the girls into town for their haircut to give you a head start."

"Oh Rose, I hate to ask you dear, after your long drive, I know you must be so tired."

"Really, I'm not tired. Please let me do this for you." Rose carried the leftovers to the fridge. "I'm a safe driver. I'm a little directionally challenged, but it's not very far is it?"

Odelia stared at Rose with her hands folded across her apron. She hesitated and settled on an answer. "All right. You're an angel you know." Laughter overtook her. "And as far as finding Trudy's, you drive down the drive way turn left at the main road and it will lead you straight into Bon Amie. I'll have a lot done when you return, and we can sit and have that chat. You can tell me everything about that loser, Ted, and your not so tactful mother."

Rose reached for a dishtowel and dried the rest of the dishes. "I'm sure you know by now I'm not very good with children, but how hard can this be? If you round up the girls, I'll go put on sandals." She took a deep breath and waited until the lump in her throat cleared. "There's not much to tell about either mom or Ted. Not much at all." Rose turned to walk away and stopped. "Aunt Odelia, speaking of mothers, where is Lizzy and Bea's mother? Is she on a trip?"

"No, honey child, she's gone. Left those two girls like they were never part of her. Never looked back. Went to find herself, she said. That was over two years ago, almost three. Broke Sam's heart and shattered Bea. Being only two when Lisa left, Lizzy acts like she doesn't remember much. But I think she remembers plenty. She knows something is missing, that much I'm sure of."

Wiping her eyes with the corner of her apron, she shook her head. "If you give me your keys I'll have one of the boys take the rest of your stuff out of your car and make room for those two."

"Okay, thanks." Rose got lost for a moment in her thoughts. Once again she could see Sam's disapproving look from this morning. "I would imagine it's hard to tell when Sam is upset or not. He always seems upset."

Odelia's face held a sad smile. "Rose, *cher*, you've got Sam all wrong. He's a serious man. That he is, but he doesn't have a mean bone in him. He's just a man afraid to trust and bound and determined that nothing will hurt his family again. That scowl hides a lot of hurt, but he has his moments. I couldn't have loved any boys of my own like I love these five boys."

"Five? You mean there's more?" Rose eyes widened with surprise. "I only remember three."

"The twins, Rusty and Randy. They were probably at camp, when you were here. Now they are all grown up and are away at their first year of college." Odelia wiped the counter top one more time. "They are all men now, but they will always be those little boys that needed me so when their mom died. Sam needed me more than the rest. I think he feels deeper than some people. More than people give him credit. I'll tell you about him sometime. There is more to that man. A lot more."

CHAPTER TWO

Rose rushed downstairs to find Lizzy and Bea swinging on the front porch. Lizzy smiled a timid smile clutching her doll and Bea scowled, and said, "We've been waiting."

"Now you girls mind your manners and don't give Rose any trouble. Tell Trudy I'll see her later in the week." Aunt Odelia bent over and gave Lizzy a big hug. She gave her attention to Bea. "Come on Bea, smile, I promise it won't break your sweet face," she said as she hugged her and winked at Rose.

"I don't understand why she has to take us. Daddy can drive us later." The sullen girl made eye contact with Rose. "I know daddy would like to see Trudy." A small smirk crossed her face.

"Behave, Bea, you know what your dad said. He has a lot on his mind and besides it'll be fun riding in that car." Odelia patted Rose's hand. "Thanks again, Hon, you're a godsend."

Rose hurried to her car speaking to Lizzy and Bea as she got in. "Who wants to ride in the front?"

"Lizzy can't ride in the front if you have an air bag. Don't you know that?" Bea asked. "We'll both sit in the back." With that said the two girls crawled into the back seat and Bea buckled Lizzy and then herself.

"Wished I'd thought of that." Rose drove down the lane toward the road. What was she doing finding the need to argue with a little girl? She was the grown up and she was not going to let a little girl get her down, not on a day full of sunshine as this one. "Aunt Odelia said to turn to the left and keep going until the road ran slap dab into town. Is that right?"

"Yes ma'am," said Lizzy. Rose looked in her rear view mirror at Bea, who sat very straight with her lips pressed tightly together. A child that was old beyond her years.

The silence drove her crazy. *I'm so bad at this.* She tried desperately to think of something to say. What did one talk about with children? Especially the one that didn't want to hear anything she had to say.

"Are both of you in school?" she asked.

"School hasn't started yet." Bea look of discuss further set Rose in her place. "And Lizzy is too young."

"Really. I went to school ever since I could remember, year round. My school was a boarding school in South Carolina." Rose's memories of those days still caused her anxiety. She should have known normal kids in normal families lived with their parents and attended regular school.

"Did you really write a book? Or did you make that up, too?" Bea asked.

Rose took in a deep breath. At last a question from Bea. "Yes." Here was something she could talk about, she relaxed. "In fact I have written many books, but I've only sold four of them so far."

"Do they have pictures?" asked Lizzy.

"No, I write books for grown-ups."

After what seemed like hours, they rounded a curve and like Aunt Odelia said ran right onto the Main street, of Bon Amie. The town had changed very little from what she remembered. A tree lined street with store fronts on both side. Some stores had rockers on the walkway some had benches where people sat and visited. Slowing down, Rose looked for Trudy's salon.

"Stop the car! That's Trudy's shop, Miss Rose," Lizzy shrieked.

Rose slammed on her breaks causing the two passengers in the back seat to lunge forward.

"Good grief," yelled Bea.

"Are the two of you okay? I'm so sorry, girls, Lizzy startled me." Rose's insides shook. "Wait, please let me park the car."

She had barely turned the car off when Bea had the seat belts undone and the door opened and she all but pulled Lizzy out of the car.

"We're going inside, where it's safe," Bea said.

Rose rested her head on the steering wheel for a moment. "I knew I wasn't good with kids. Maybe I should never be trusted with them to my care," she whispered to the heavens.

Closing the car door, she at the storefront. The large hand painted sign read "Hair Today Gone Tomorrow." The letters popped out with their bright red color that sported white daisies intertwined against a black background.

Surprise crossed her face as she opened the door into the strangest looking beauty salon she'd ever seen. Two salon chairs stood in front of a floor to ceiling mirror. Plants, pots, and an assortment of ribbons lined shelves along the opposite wall. A door, so short that one had to stoop to get, in opened and out walked a cute little brunette. The first thing Rose noticed about the woman was her smile, so friendly and real. Rose liked the feel of the business. A place ready for just about anything. Just like the owner.

"Come in, come in. The girls told me about the ride you gave them to town. Pull up a chair and keep me company while I shave two heads." The petite woman with large bosoms and bigger hair, stood with an arm around both girls.

"Hi, I'm Trudy Thibodeaux. You must be Rose?" Trudy said in a deep husky voice. "Odelia called and told me you would bring these two rag mops in for a trim." She let Lizzy and Bea go and gently shoved them to the back of the store. "Girls put on those old shirts you like to wear." Trudy cleared a basket of blue ribbons off a chair and motioned for Rose to sit.

Rose couldn't keep her lips from settling on a smile as Trudy teased and hugged the two girls as she cut their hair. "Lizzy, is Miss Abby getting her hair cut today?" Trudy held Lizzy's doll up and examined her hair.

"No, her hair doesn't grow." Lizzy giggled, and then retrieved her doll and sat Miss Abby in her lap. "She's going to watch."

The closeness between the three was apparent. Bea and Lizzy's face lit up as they chattered with Trudy with such ease. The three of them held a special history, of that Rose was sure.

As she observed Sam's daughters, Rose once again was struck with the knowledge that neither of the girls had his eyes. What color were his eyes anyway? Were they a faded blue or a steel gray with a splash of green? The color was a mystery but the story buried deep in his eyes intrigued her. They seemed to hold in check all his hurts and disappointments. Had his wife caused all his pain, or was it someone else?

"Rose?" Trudy called. "Boy you were way off somewhere. Do you want to be next?" Trudy stood back and cocked her head from one side to the other. "I could cut it in a style that would free those curls that keep trying to escape."

Rose quickly shook her head. "No, I better wait until I go into the city." She caught herself and looked up to see if she had offended Trudy, but the woman's face still held that I want to be your friend look.

"I'm sorry. It's just that my mother would never approve of me letting my curls loose. I better not."

Looking around the shop, Trudy eyes lit with mischief. "Is your mother here? I don't see her, do you?" Trudy put a bow in Lizzy's hair and lifted her down from the chair. "Okay you two beauties deserve a treat, how about you go to Miller's drug store and get each of you a soda and be sure to tell Miss Maude all your family secrets. Come right back when you finished."

Lizzy planted a big kiss on Trudy's cheek and glanced at Rose, and then tucked her chin down, and turned a light pink. Bea grabbed her hand and they ran out the door, giggling all the way down the sidewalk.

"Those two just tug at your heart, don't they?" Trudy said.

"You know what, Trudy? If you have time I will have that cut. You're right, my mother is not here to criticize and it is my hair." Rose sat in the seat and made eye contact with Trudy in the mirror. "Cut away, Trudy, cut away."

"You can't rush a master piece." Trudy put oil in her hand and started to message Rose's head as she talked. "So how long are you planning to stay?"

"I don't know yet. I guess it depends how long I'm welcome. Do you mind if I ask you a personal question?"

"Honey, in a small town. There are no personal questions."

"Are you and Sam, you know, an item? The two of you talk so fondly about each other and anyone can see how crazy the girls are about you."

Trudy stopped massaging and grinned. "So, you're sweet on Sam. Well don't worry about me." A grin as big as Trudy's hair spread across her face. "At one time, I would have loved nothing more than to have one of the LeBlanc brothers take a liking to me, but they were slow as molasses. So I moved on and met my honey at the Cajun festival, right here in Bon Amie. He asked me to dance and one week later he asked me to marry him. That man was never one to let moss grow under his feet. He's away on an oil rig, but he'll be home in two weeks."

Trudy washed her hands in the sink and returned to Rose. "So if you want to go for Sam, go for it."

Heat crept up Rose's body and settled in her face. "Mercy me, I'm not sweet on Sam. I don't even know him, and besides I don't want another man. Not now. Probably not ever."

"Don't get excited. It's okay. The more you know me, the more you'll know that you would have to slap me backwards to offend me."

The shampooing led to more conversation, mostly from Trudy. Rose loved her accent and the way she threw southern sayings into her sentences. Back in the chair, the sound of Trudy's scissors clicked in an even rhythm. Rose couldn't remember when she'd felt so relaxed. The head massage Trudy had given her before the shampoo made her bones feel like rubber.

"Boy that man Ted really did a number on you, didn't he?"

"How did you know? Did Aunt Odelia tell you?" Rose asked.

"No, but if you think we are out of the know here, you haven't met the Mouton sisters. Two of the sweetest women you'll ever meet but don't whisper too loud, they hear everything." She let laughter out that was infectious. "They also tell everything. Feel like it's their true gift in life to spread the news." Trudy cut a few more curls and smiled as if she was truly satisfied. "If you ever want to talk, I'm a real good listener." Trudy put the scissors down, dusted the hair off her face and neck with a large soft brush, and then she turned Rose around to the mirror.

"Wow." Rose looked up at Trudy. "Thanks. You know my mother will hate this. But I love it." Her red curls still damp bounced around her face freely.

Trudy showed her around the shop, pride in her voice she informed Rose about her unusual business. "This place is a two-fer. I cut hair for both the living and the dead. My specialties are up-do's and casket covers. I get to make people look good while they're here and I'm blessed to do the same when they say their goodbyes."

"You really do hair for dead people?" Rose asked.

"Sure. Some of my elderly clients have a standing appointment to have their hair fixed after they're gone. They want to look nice for their showing." Elbowing Rose, she added, "Sometimes that's the only time they don't complain." Trudy released her musical laughter. And had Rose laughing as well.

"Trudy, do you know the two ladies peeking in your front window?" Rose asked about the two elderly ladies, one tall with gray hair piled on top of her head, the other one short with gray curly hair, both wearing red tennis shoes.

"I was just talking about them, the famous Mouton sisters," she said between bouts of laughter. She waved at them as they turned and walked down the sidewalk. "Now Rose you've seen Bon Amie's own walking newspaper. So if you want to know anything ask them." Rose and Trudy's laughter was interrupted by the sound of little girls giggling. "I hear the girls; the sugar must have hit. Good luck driving home." Trudy said, walking Rose to the door.

The door flew open and Lizzy came running in with chocolate on her face. She came to a halt in front of Rose. "You look beautiful, Miss Rose."

"Thank you, and so do you. Why don't the two of you wash your hands and face and if you two are ready, I think we should go. Aunt Odelia will need my help. She has a lot of pie baking today." Rose waited until the girls returned and said. "Trudy, thank you and I hope we can talk again soon," She reached out her hand for a shake and Trudy pulled her in for a hug.

"Tell Odelia, I'll be out later to help, I know this is a busy time for her, and with her arm broken they've had a heck of a time finding help."

Rose couldn't hide the smile on her face as she left her new friend's place of happiness. Her steps were as light as her bouncing curls. "Do you girls need to stop anywhere in town before we head back?" Rose asked enjoying the bright sunlight and soft breeze.

"No, I need to get home. I have something to do," Bea said.

"Yeah, she wants to start a book," Lizzy chimed in.

"Shut up."

"A book? What fun, maybe I can help Bea?" Rose said.

"No, I can do it myself. It's a dumb idea anyway."

Rose put the car in gear, and they were on their way. She moved the rear view mirror so she could see Bee. "First off there are no dumb ideas. And you know writing is very fun, if you do need my help, please let me know."

Maybe I have something to offer these girls after all. Rose put the top down and allowing the sun to warm her spirits and her hair blow in the wind.

Sam strolled out of the house when they drove up, only to be met by Bea as she stormed out of the car and ran to him.

"Dad look! Look what she did. See my hair. She ruined it. Trudy had it fixed so nice, and Rose drove with the top down and messed it up."

Rose couldn't believe her ears as Bea tattled on her, her hands on her hips and her back to Rose. Bea had laughed with glee as much as Lizzy did when the wind blew in their face. Rose, amazed as Bea's tongue lashed out as many complaints as she could muster up, all the while her little hands were tightly fisted and her right foot just a patting. Rose mouth became dry and she knew she was on the verge of both laughter and tears.

"And you know what else? She thought Lizzy went to school and–"

"Enough Bea. Miss Rose was kind enough to drive you to town. Where are your manners?" Sam said, his eyes searched Rose's. Seeking what? Answers, confession, Rose was not sure.

Sam smoothed Bea's hair gently with his large hands and then turned her face up to look into his. "Besides your hair looks great, you're as pretty as a picture." The look on his face reflected not anger, but the love he felt for this very disagreeable child.

Lizzy tugged on his pants. "What about my hair, Papa? Does it look like a picture, too?"

Rose turned around to hide the disappointment and a little jealousy. No one ever loved her like that when she was a child, and she envied the look he held for his daughters. She'd never known what it was like to have a dad, not a real one anyway. The dozen or so men in her Mom's life didn't count; they came and went like the seasons. No matter, she put shoulders back and stood straighter, she wasn't a child any longer. She didn't need anyone to love her to make her happy. She had decided that a long time ago. Happiness would have to come from her.

"I'm sorry if they hurt your feelings, Rose," Sam said.

Rose hadn't heard him approach until he spoke. "You are as quiet as a cat and have a habit of sneaking up on me."

"Excuse me, but for your information I don't sneak."

"I didn't mean. What I wanted to say was_. Oh never mind." She bit her lower lip to keep from saying more of nothing. To be a lover of words, she never had the right ones handy to use when she needed them.

Sam cocked his head to one side and watched her face for a moment. He seemed to choose his words very carefully. "Why do you do that?"

"Do what?"

"Start to say something and then hold it back."

"What I usually have to say is not important and no one wants to hear a bunch of nonsense."

"Whoever told you that, Rose, was wrong. Everyone has the right to say whatever he or she thinks. You might be surprised who would listen." Sam waited before he left. His gaze

"Hey, thank you for taking my girls. That really helped me out, and not to mention the time it gave Odelia." A smile flew across his face and stilled her heart." But, Bea is right you should not have driven with the top down. Not safe you know." With a wink, he added, "You look like a picture too, Rose." Sam jiggled his keys and whistled as he ambled toward his truck.

Rose feet wouldn't move as she blatantly stared as his backside climb into his truck and drove away. Basking in his words she decided it was time to find her Aunt and get her mind off that confusing man.

Odelia called out when she heard Rose come in the kitchen. Hey, I knew I heard your steps I would give you a big hug but as you can see I'm up to my elbows in flour.

Rose rounded the table and gave Odelia a small hug.

"Rose you look absolutely beautiful. I love your haircut it suits you. Why don't you change and keep me company? You can tell me everything." Odelia put down the ball of dough she was forming and took Rose's new look in. A smile one could tell she gave out freely. "Honey, you'll never know how happy you've made me by being here. Now hurry back I've been waiting all morning to hear about that uptight sister of mine."

Rose changed into old comfortable jeans and a tee shirt, all of which her mother hated, and glanced in the mirror at the curls bouncing on her head. Picking up the beat she bounced down the stairs, her gait light and free.

She washed her hands at the sink and replied. "I'll be glad to share my pitiful life with you but only if you allow me to help. I'm not the most graceful in the kitchen, but I so love to bake." She looked around at the dough and the couple of bowls around her aunt. "What are we making?"

"That darn Preston can sweet talk me into anything. I have six pies to bake, but he didn't know that and he begged me for sweet dough fig pies." Her love for those boys could be heard in her voice and with her actions through food.

Her aunt dusted the large cutting board with flour. Her hands moving as the pro she was. "I can't say no to these boys. They get to hugging on me and sweet talking, and before I know it I'm doing just what I said I wouldn't do. That boy so loves to eat." She took a drink out of the large glass of ice tea sitting in front of her. "I know they all love food, but my Preston has a love affair with every bite he eats. Pour yourself a glass of sweet tea, and I'll show you how to make fig pies."

Aunt Odelia punched and pulled the dough into small circles then rolled them out flat in an effortless movement. Rose tried her hand at the process, but her dough had a mind of its own, and soon holes appeared and seemed to grow. "What did I tell you? I'm not very graceful in the kitchen."

"Never you mind, Hon, you come behind me and spoon the filling in, then I'll show you how to fold and seal them. Tell me, Rose, how's your mom?"

"The same, I'm sorry to say. She has a new man now; this one's richer. So of course she's happy for awhile." Rose wiped her hands to remove the flour and began spooning the fig mixture onto the dough her aunt had rolled.

"As far as my failed wedding. According to mom, it was my fault. All my fault. You know the same old, same old. 'If I had been more he wouldn't have left me,' she said. She leaned her hip against the table and thought for a moment. "You know, I don't know how to be more. I try. In the end, I'm still just me, and we all know that's not nearly enough."

Odelia shook her flour-covered finger at Rose. "You listen to me, you don't have to be anything else to please people. What and who you are is more than enough. Don't let Ruth tell you any different. She's one of those people that wouldn't know how to be content if it killed her. Her idea of being successful is how much expensive stuff you have and the famous people you pretend to know. You know she wouldn't be happy if she was the only hen in a chicken yard full of roosters." Her aunt took a deep breath, "be yourself, Rose, it's the best part of who you are."

Was that pity on her aunt's face? That was just what she didn't want.

"I'm sorry Aunt Odelia. For the life of me, I have never understood how the two of you are sisters. Two women couldn't be more different. I didn't mean to make you sad. I'm fine. You know I learned a long time ago Ruth and I will never be close, and I'm okay." She heaved a heavy sigh and offered a weak laugh. "Let's talk about you, what you've been doing and tell me all about this family you take such loving care of."

Peace returned to Odelia face as she began to tell stories about her boys. "I tell you they are something, each and every one of them so different. Lewis, the oldest, is the strong silent type. When he and Susan got married and moved into the Gray House I thought we wouldn't see much of him anymore. But I was wrong, that short trip across the field has turned into a well-worn path. Of course, since she's pregnant and confined to bed-rest we don't see much of her right now. In fact, after these are baked, I thought we would walk over and bring her a few. You'll love Susan, and I know she wants to meet you."

"Will she and the baby be all right?" Rose asked.

"I think so, hon. She's a stubborn girl and usually gets what she sets a mind to. Lewis never had a chance when she set her hat for him. But you know you couldn't ask for a better match."

"What about Sam, Aunt Odelia? You said you would tell me more about him." Rose felt her face flush. Must be the heat from the oven.

"He's the worrier. That boy worries about everyone, even people who don't deserve his concern. Now his choice of a wife was not a good match. Not from the beginning. He married Lisa when Bea was three years old. Sam fell in love with that little girl as much as he fell in love with Lisa. Adopted her as soon as they were married, and has been a real dad to her as much as he has to his own blood, Lizzy."

"That takes a real commitment and a lot of love to take a child that you had nothing to do with her conception and make her feel like she belonged," Rose whispered.

Odelia face lit up. "What it really takes is a real man with a heart as big as the one my Sam has. It was so hard watching him try to make Lisa content, but she was much like your mom." Odelia opened the oven, and Rose put the two large pans off completed fig pies on the racks.

"One day, right after Lizzy turned two, she up and skipped town. Sam found a letter telling him that he and the girls were smothering her. Not to mention the rest of his family. I'm afraid we were all a little too much for her." Odelia shook her head and rubbed her arm in the sling. "The note said she felt as if she had lost herself. She needed and deserved more, so much more than what Sam had to offer."

The kitchen filled with the most wonderful smell as the little pies baked. Rose watched as her Aunt took the finished pies out of the oven and sprinkled them with sugar. Rose had to wipe her mouth; she felt like she was drooling.

"Did he go after her?" she asked.

"Not at first. He was too hurt, embarrassed, or just plain mad. When he decided to look for her, he hired someone, but after six months and lots of money paid out, she couldn't be found. Can you imagine walking away from a man like Sam? And those girls, her own little girls. She just walked away from those babies like they were nothing. Never looked back, never called, just washed her hands of them."

"So he's still married."

"Until he catches up with her, he can't get a divorce. He's caught in limbo."

A knock on the front door stilled Rose's unanswered questions on her lips.

"Where are you Odelia? Like I didn't know," Trudy called.

Rose was glad to see her new friend, but sorry the story about Sam was over.

"Hey lady. My, what cute hair." Trudy sat two pie plates down on the counter top and poured herself a glass of tea. "I went ahead and made two pies at home before I came. Both chocolate if that's okay? And I met MaeMae in town she ask me to come by and pick up a big pot of Shrimp Jambalaya, and Possum sent twenty pounds of fresh caught shrimp he'd cleaned.

"Oh, sweet Lord. I just love the folks of Bon Amie they are special." Odelia turned to Rose. "You remember my cousin, MaeMae?"

"Was she the lady you took me too when that cut I had got infected?"

"Yes, she's the town healer. I thought you would remember her. And Possum is the guy that lives on the boat. He's a great fisherman with a big heart."

"Oh, I put the shrimp in the big freezer on the back porch, and MaeMae also sent more tea for the swelling in your arm. I hope the pies are good," Trudy said.

"Honey, you could have made mud pies and those boys would never notice. But they do love chocolate. Rose and I are about to walk over to the Gray House and see Susan, want to come?"

"Sure, is she feeling all right?" Trudy asked.

"I hope so. Lewis didn't say anything different at breakfast, and to tell you the truth after I saw my Rose I just forgot to ask," Odelia confessed.

Heading out the door as Sam rounded the corner and ran right into Rose. She fell against the doorframe, and Sam fell against her, banging her head onto the wall.

Sam was quick to right himself but still held onto Rose's arm. "Are you all right?" he asked, his eyes searched her face for an answer.

"Yes. I'm fine," she said rubbing her head.

Sam held eye contact, and Rose tried to look away, but she couldn't break the spell.

Trudy broke the moment when she cleared her throat.

Sam let go of Rose's arm and lowered his eyes. "Hi Trudy."

"Hi Sam, before I forget, Possum said he'll stop by later today and get your harvest schedule. Said he had some free time and that he and that guy Joelette married, Mansir, would like to help."

"I would like to have the help, that's for sure," Sam said.

"Where are you going in such a hurry, Sam?" Odelia asked.

A frown creased his face. "Those damn boys. Just wait until I get my hands on them. The sheriff just called, and he's holding Rusty and Randy until I can pay their fine. Rusty got another ticket." He glanced back at Rose then turned to Odelia. "Got to go, tell Lewis I'll be back, if I'm not back when Possum gets here, have Lewis talk with him, and be sure to tell him thanks."

"The twins are home? You weren't expecting them to come in for the harvest were you?" Odelia asked.

"No, I guess they decided to leave the University early." He threw his hands up in the air. "Who knows what happened with those two? I gave up a long time ago." Sam tipped his cap. "Ladies, I'll see you later."

"Sam sure was shook up. Seemed more flustered to me than usual." Trudy looked at Rose with a strange grin on her face.

"It's the red hair, shakes men up all the time," Rose said.

Bea ran toward Odelia and screeched to a halt in front of her. "Uncle Preston said that Lizzy and I can help him feed the new calf, can we please?" she begged.

"Okay, but tell him that we'll be at Uncle Lewis's house for a while, so if he needs to do something to drop you both there."

Bea glanced at Rose her face free of the joy that she'd just shown.

"That girl just doesn't like me," Rose said as she watched Bea meet up with Lizzy.

"Honey, she's not one that likes change. That little girl has been through a lot, and she never gives trust freely. She's been disappointed too many times I guess. Sam wasn't her mother's only man."

Odelia put her hand across her waist. "Well, two more for dinner so I better throw more potatoes in the salad, and add water to the gumbo. It's a shame that Babette's Tea Room isn't open yet in *Bon Amie* I would buy two more pies. Oh well I did make quite a few fried pies, that will have to do."

Rose enjoyed the chatter between Odelia and Trudy. Every now and then she chimed in. This must be what it was like to have friends you felt comfortable with. Something she'd never had. One boarding school after another, she was always the third girl out. This was nice, very nice.

The Gray House loomed in the distance, a white one-story home with a wraparound porch, like arms embracing the house. Dark green ferns hung from the eaves and white rockers graced the porch waiting patiently for the cool evening breeze. Enormous round columns supported the red roof and grand stately steps led to double red front doors with pots of miniature roses adorned each step.

"Why is this house called the Gray house? I don't see a speck of gray anywhere," asked Rose.

"It was built by Gray LeBlanc many years ago, and the name stuck. There is quite a history to this house as well as the big house. Get Sam to tell you. He is a stickler for details. Especially about this house."

She opened the door and walked into a hallway that led to a sun porch with white wicker furniture and crisp floral cushions in bright yellow and white stripes.

On a chaise lounge covered in a light throw laid a dark hair beauty of a woman heavy with child.

"Odelia, Trudy, how nice to see you both this morning. And you must be the famous Rose that caused such a ruckus this morning at the big house. Lewis told me about it when he came home for his gloves."

Rose couldn't help but notice the gleam of excitement in Susan's eye as the woman pushed herself to a more sitting position. For being banished to bed all day, she had a wonderful attitude.

"It's time someone shook up these men. Please have a seat." Susan gestured to a chair close to her. "I have a million questions."

"You sure look pretty today Susan. We brought you a couple of warm fig pies; I'll get you a cup of decaf to wash it down." Odelia fussed over her like a queen.

"Later I'll brush your hair and put it up for you, how does that sound?" asked Trudy.

"Trudy, as always, you read my mind. You know where everything is in my room. Thank you so much."

Susan turned to Rose as the other two women left the room. "Tell me all about yourself. Since I've been confined to this bed, I miss all the girl talk except when Odelia gets a chance to visit. You must live a very exciting life, being a writer and all."

"Not really, writing is a solitary job. It's just the computer, my characters and me most of the time. Don't get me wrong I love what I do. I don't know any other job I would rather be doing. I have stories and characters running around my head all the time. I love storytelling. Most of all, I love to give the characters a happy ending. That's why I write fiction." Rose took a deep breath. She loved to talk about writing, and sometimes she talked too much.

It was hard to keep herself in check. She looked at Susan, half expecting the look of boredom on her face, but she still looked excited.

"I read romance books along with women's fiction. Maybe it's because I enjoy a good ending to a story. It all sounds very fascinating to me. How in the world you are able to create characters and plots just baffles me. And the happy endings are a part of life, and that's what makes them special."

"I have to disagree with you there, Susan. I have not met anyone in real life that has experienced a happy ending."

Susan's face changed from excitement to sadness. "You know, Rose, you've just not met the right people."

"Maybe." Rose sighed. "Enough about me. Tell me, when are you due?"

Susan's answer died on her lips as Odelia and Trudy entered the room laughing. Trudy carried a tray of cups and the four women shared coffee, pie and talk. Rose could not remember a more enjoyable hour in her life.

Goodbyes shared, Rose promised Susan she would return for a longer visit, and she agreed to bring her one of her books.

The heat of the day bore down on the three women as they made their way back to the big house. "I could use a cold glass of sweet tea before I make a cake. I can't have my babies returning home without something special. And I have to find the girls, it is way past time they rest awhile before dinner." Odelia said.

"Does Sam still need someone to stay with the girls during harvest? You know I would if I could," Trudy said.

Odelia shook her head yes. "But now that the twins are home, he can at least stop worrying about hiring a lot of field hands, but I don't think he's had any luck with a sitter for the girls."

"What about you Rose?" Trudy asked.

"Me? I would love to help, of course, but I don't know the first thing about kids. Besides, neither of them like me very much. And I think I need to help Aunt Odelia. I'm sorry."

Her aunt put an arm around her. "Don't you worry, Rose, no one will make you do anything you are not comfortable doing." Trudy said her goodbyes, and Aunt Odelia went looking for the girls. Rose took the time to check her email.

The door to her bedroom was half opened. Bea and Lizzy were in her room. Bea sat on the floor looking at one of her books. Lizzy was playing with her globe. Rose's special globe.

Panic sized her, freezing her vocal cords. She snatched the snow globe out of Lizzy's hands. The little girl flashed the same scared look Rose had witnessed just this morning.

"She wasn't hurting that old thing. You didn't have to rip it out of her hands, you know." Bea said.

"I'm sorry, Lizzy, I know you were being careful but you don't touch other people's things unless you ask. And who gave either of you permission to come into my room without me here?" Rose's hands trembled as she sat the globe down on the mantle out of the reach of Lizzy.

"I sorry, Miss Rose. I just wanted to see what the little people were doing in the ball.

Lizzy's lips quivered and Rose knew that it was a matter of time before a full wail would develop.

"Look girls, let's call a truce. Do you know what that is?" Rose ignored the glare Bea gave her and focused on Lizzy.

"It's kind of an agreement. I will be glad to show you all my things with the understanding that you will not enter my room without an invitation. Agreed?"

"You don't have anything we want to see. Come on, Lizzy, Let's go see what's for dinner," Bea said.

"No, I want to see the ball and hear the story. Please."

"Suit yourself. I'm going to eat." Bea walked out the door.

As soon as Bea left the room, she was back. She sat in the chair by the door. "I have to wait for Lizzy, so don't take all day."

Rose turned away so Bea could not see the smile on her face. Bea was not as cold a little girl as she pretended. She wanted to know about Rose as much as Lizzy, but didn't want anyone to know. Well she was up to the challenge, and Rose was a pro at hiding feelings.

She picked up the globe and sat on the plush rag rug at the foot of her bed. Lizzy sat beside her. Her large eyes were waiting in anticipation. Rose held the globe up to the sunlight and turned it so the snowfall of glitter and snow fell all over the smiling couple. The pair stood outside of a picket fence that guarded a walkway to a small little home with green shutters and a red roof.

"This was given to me by my fiancé when I was young. He said this was the two of us standing outside our home." Rose spoke in the same sad tone she always had when she thought of Billy, her first love. The only man that had ever loved her back.

"Why are you so sad? Did he go away? " Lizzy's little face lit up with questions as she looked into Rose's eyes and lowered her voice to a whisper. "Did he leave you like our mama did?" Lizzy asked.

Rose's insides began to shake. She put her hand on her stomach and continued. "No, Lizzy, he died a long time ago. And it still makes me a little sad when I think of him. This globe means a lot to me. I don't think I could bear it if this globe got broken. It's my happy ever after."

Lizzy reached up and patted Rose's face with her chubby little hand. "It's okay, Miss Rose. I won't break it."

Rose looked up to see Sam standing in the doorway. Watching. A shiver ran up her back. Did he always have to peer into her soul, especially when it was bare like now?

"Lizzy, Bea, Odelia is looking for you. She has your dinner ready. Go wash up and eat."

Sam never broke eye contact with her, even when the girls ran out the door. Why did he make her feel this way, always on the defensive? Well not this time. She stood tall and met him stare to stare.

In a voice not quite as strong as she intended, she said, "I did nothing wrong Sam."

A frown wrinkled his forehead and he focused on her mouth.

Rose fought the urge to reach up and wipe her lips with her hand, but instead quickly licked them.

Sam inhaled sharply and allowed a slow grin to spread across his face. "No one said you did, Rose."

Not knowing what to do next and not willing to permit him the upper hand, Rose rushed pass Sam and hurried out the door to the safety of the downstairs.

CHAPTER THREE

Bea and Lizzy talked Odelia into allowing them to eat on the gallery, which pleased Rose as she joined them.

The screen door slammed behind Sam as he walked out with a fig pie in his hand. He waved it at the women and walked down the steps toward the barn.

Rose sat back and enjoyed the view. After all, she was a healthy young woman, she reminded herself. He did have one of the best walking away views she'd ever seen. Sam's Wranglers fit his rear just right. Tight in all the right places.

He walked straight and confident in his own skin, like this is where he belonged. This man knew what he wanted and heaven help anyone that would get in his way. Rose wished she had just a tiny portion of that confidence.

"Rose, are you all right?" Aunt Odelia asked.

"Daydreaming, just daydreaming. This gumbo is great," Rose said as she took her first bite. At least while she chewed that silly grin couldn't work itself back onto her face.

The evening flew by. Rose helped cook and bake with Odelia until she thought there could not possibly be anything else to cook in the state of Louisiana.

"We will freeze this pot of shrimp gumbo and the rest of the pies and cakes until we have a full crew for the harvest. Thank goodness we had the chicken and okra gumbo made for our dinner tonight." Odelia gestured to all of the containers of food, labeled with contents and dates. "You have never seen men eat as much as these guys. We need dishes that fill them up and are easy to transport to the screened in shed closer to the fields. This helps if I have most of the main dishes prepared ahead of time."

They carried the dishes and placed them into two of the three upright freezers.

"How long will harvest last?" Rose asked.

"Depends on the equipment, the help, and barring no other trouble, about two weeks or a little more. The time spent working next to each other really pulls everyone together. Sam and his brothers will be picking and sparring the whole time. They're very close and for some reason harvest time brings them together.

Loud voices could be heard coming from the barn. "Bringing them closer couldn't come to soon by the sound of the arguing headed our way." Rose said.

"They're not arguing, Hon, that's there love language." Odelia "Well I'm going to take me a good soaking bath. I'll come by and tell you goodnight before I turn in."

Rose moved the work she'd finished to the foot of the bed. She was exhausted, and before she got ready for her bath, she needed to rest her eyes for a short time. Never had she been a part of so much cooking. She'd chopped, stirred, measured and mixed until she thought her hands would fall off. Her eyes began to feel heavy and as soon as she closed them she went to sleep.

A soft knock on her door startled Rose from a sound sleep.

"Hey girly, are you all ready in bed? Are you all right?" Preston called out from the other side of the door.

"I'm fine, what is everyone doing?"

"Just sitting around and visiting. You sure you're all right?"

"No really, give me a minute and I'll be right there." Rose straightened her top and ran her fingers through her hair. "Good enough," she said and bounded out the door.

Like Preston had reported, everyone was seated in the family room. All eyes turned to her direction, causing the warmth to slowly rise up her neck and cover her face. She missed seeing Lewis at the table, but two new faces grinned at her. Younger versions of Sam, but both much larger in size. Out of the corner of her eyes she caught Sam gesturing to his face. Was he waving? Or did she have something on her face? Rose ran her fingers over her left cheek. Sam shook his head and gestured to the other side. There, she removed a hot pink Post-it note, she crumbled the note and stashed it in her pocket.

With all of the men hiding smiles and holding back laughter she rounded her shoulders and stared them down. "What? Hot pink not your color?" she asked then took her seat. Laughter rang out across the room. Could that possibly be a grin on Sam's face? Was it aimed at her? Rose looked Sam straight in the eye and winked. And immediately lost her breath. Why, praise be, did she do that? To recover, she turned to the first twin on her left, took a deep breath and jumped in.

"I don't believe we've met, my name is Rose."

"Name is Rusty, ma'am, and we already know your name. Odelia talks non-stop about you. You sure are a little thing, but I bet you pack a mighty punch. The ugly one over there is my twin brother Randy. As you can see I got all the looks."

Randy reached over and offered his hand to Rose. "Yeah, but I got all the brains, little brother. Welcome."

Rose looked back and forth between the two, and for the life of her could not tell them apart. "Thank you guys. I think you have the prettiest eyes, Randy, but you have the strongest chin, Rusty."

The table once again broke into laughter. She had scored again. Stealing a quick glance at Sam, she thought she saw a hint of approval. Then he turned his attention to his brothers. Loud voices and laughter soon filled the room again.

After the dishes were done, Aunt Odelia excused herself for a quick bath. Rose headed outside to take a breather and get her head on straight but was soon intercepted by Sam.

"Rose, the boys are going to play forty two and wanted to know if you would like to join them?"

Rose shoved her hands in her jean pockets. "Maybe later, let me sit a little. What is forty two anyway?"

"A domino game, it's not hard to learn." Sam turned to leave and stopped. "Could you step into my office for a moment? I have a business proposition I would like for you to hear." With an after-thought, he added, "I'll even let you sit a spell in there as we talk."

The office turned out as grand as the rest of the house. It smelled of leather and lemon oil. A giant picture of two men and three women standing beside the Plantation home hung above the fireplace. Sam resembled the older man. On closer investigation, it was the eyes and the way they both held their lips so tight. Much like they were holding something they wanted to say at bay.

"That's my great great-grandfather and his brother, they built all of this.

The two women standing by their sides are their wives and the other woman their sister. Some time, if you're interested, I'll tell you their story, but right now I need to ask you something." Sam motioned for her to sit, but she remained standing.

Now what had she done. She thought she handled the situation with the globe as tactful as she could. "If this is about this afternoon, Sam, I—."

"What? No, I wanted to ask you if you would be interested in a job? Hear me out before you ask questions. I need to hire someone to help Odelia. She wouldn't ask for help if she was on her death bed, but I can see she's in need." Sam picked up a letter opener on his desk and began to fiddle with it. "This would have to be our secret. Odelia would have a fit if she knew I'd asked you. You could look in on my girls when you weren't too busy. Are you interested?" His question lingered I the air as Rose held her breath. "You said you were not busy for the next month."

Rose twisted her hands trying to decide if she should break her promise to her aunt.

"Well you might be surprised, but that is one of the main reasons I came. Aunt Odelia asked me if I could give her a little help." Rose shook her head and faced Sam. "Of course, knowing my aunt, she was trying to get me out of Atlanta and away from my embarrassing situation." Rose began to pace. "I don't think of this as a job, but more as family helping family. But as far as looking in on your girls, they don't even like me. And I know nothing about what kids like to do. I don't know.

"Rose, I..."

Rose held her hand up to stop him and began to pace around the room again. "But, I can't say no. Not after you opened your home to me. I guess for four weeks I could do anything. Oh, I don't know. What do you think?" Rose stopped pacing and chewed her lower lip as she searched Sam's face for an answer.

"It's not that big of a decision. The girls really are not much trouble, and everyone keeps an eye on them, but to have someone in charge, you know would ease my mind." He gave her that long stare. "Never mind. I certainly don't want to be the cause of you having a tizzy."

"Wait, first, I never have had a tizzy, or do I ever plan to have one. I guess I could do this, but I will not accept pay. After all, I'm staying under your roof and eating your food. And I would do anything for my Aunt. No pay and that's final."

"I insist. If you are under my employment then when I need to instruct you on how to do something it won't be awkward."

"That is a prime example of why I will not except pay. I'm through letting men tell me what to do." Rose's voice swelled louder.

They stood, her with hands on her hips, and Sam with his hands flat on the desk. Neither blinked.

A slow grin twitched at Sam's lips. "All right, you win this one. But only because I have no other choice." Sam opened the door and headed out, but muttered. "I knew you and your red hair were trouble.

Damn that woman. For being so small, she sure was feisty. Sam knew that most of her barks were a defense tactic. She was as vulnerable as a newborn kitten. Her wide green eyes begged for attention and understanding. And the way she threw that perky little nose in the air when she wanted to make a point was unnerving. But it was her mouth that he had a hard time not staring at when she was near. The desire to kiss her increased daily as he found himself close to her.

This was the not the time for him to all of a sudden be drawn to another woman. He thought after Lisa had deserted him he was finished with women. But his mind and body told him different.

That little mole at the corner of those full lips needed kissing. Kissed right and often. Well, he didn't need to be interested in another woman. He'd been fooled before. He would keep this strictly business. There was no denying the fact she had a way of getting under his skin.

Rose woke in panic. Oh God, what was today? She jumped out of bed and searched frantically for her day planner. What good was a planner that she kept all her deadlines in if she never knew where to find it? Taking time off was one thing, but life didn't just stand still, her book wouldn't write itself.

She ran across the room, her heart beating so hard she was sure it was going to jump right out of her chest.

"I'm a failure at everything I've tried but not this. Not this, please not this," she muttered. Writing was her life and she was good at it. Even most critics thought so. She would not mess this up. Even if she was having the best time she'd ever had with this funny family. She'd have to do something today and try to get back on some kind of schedule. She would have to distance herself from this place for a while.

After breakfast, Rose called a hotel in Lafayette and booked the next three nights.

"Aunt Odelia, I have to go away for a few days. You did say your work wouldn't start again until the beginning of next week. I promise to be back on Sunday afternoon to give you and the girls my undivided attention." She let out the breath she'd been holding. "I have a deadline that crept up on me that I have to meet. I can't believe I allowed this to happen." Rose's voice slid into a quieter tone as she took her Aunt's hand in hers. "Please tell me I'm not putting you in a bind."

"Don't you think another thing about it, Rose Do what you have to do and come back to us as soon as you can. I'll tell Sam and we'll make do until you return." Odelia pulled Rose into one of her tight hugs.

"Thanks, Aunt Odelia, I knew you would understand. I've already packed my car I'm not taking much, so if it's all right, I'll leave the rest in my room? I stacked everything out of sight in the wardrobe."

"Let me fix you a little care package so you can be on your way."

Armed with a box full of fried pies, cookies, and sandwiches, Rose kissed Odelia and rushed to her car. She paused and glanced back at the house that now held a special place in her heart. There stood Bea and Lizzy watching from the safety of the windows of Bea's bedroom. Rose waved. But the curtains closed and the girls disappeared out of sight. Her aunt had followed her and squeezed Rose's arm.

"Don't worry, Rose, I'll tell them why you had to leave. Everything will be fine." Her aunt gave her one last hug and kissed her cheek.

Rose's day and nights were filled with work, but for some reason she couldn't pull the real story out of this book. She knew her process by now and usually had some problems with the first draft, but this time the story just wasn't there. Even her characters were unlikable, and characters were always her strong suit.

Rose laid back on the bed, and her mind drifted to the what could be happening at the plantation. Were Bea and Lizzy running thought the house playing spy kids? Or were they stuck to the TV? Did Odelia really need her help and she had bailed? What were those brothers up too? She missed playing cards or dominos with them at night. But most of all, she missed their talks and teasing. Rose sat up and laughed out loud. "And I miss your morning news from Bon Amie, Preston. The Mouton sisters always had great news, better than any of the tabloids."

For the first time in her writing career, Rose picked up the phone and called her editor. She needed more research and she needed to re-plot, and maybe the research was within her reach from the plantation and news from Bon Amie. But what Rose needed most was time.

###

"Papa, Rose is gone," Lizzy said.

"What do you mean Rose is gone? I'm sure she's around somewhere. Maybe she went to visit Susan," replied Sam.

"Unh-unh, we saw her leave in her car." Lizzy took a deep breath before continuing. "She had a suitcase and her room is cleaned out. She's gone." Big tears fell from Lizzy's eyes. "I think I made her mad like I made Mommy. I sorry, Papa." She gulped.

"Come here, sweet pea." Sam gathered Lizzy in his arms. "Now you listen to me. No one left because of anything you or Bea did. Do you understand?

Remember when your Mom went away? We talked a lot about why. Don't you ever think that again, okay?"

Sam could feel his temper rising. "Bea, is all this correct? Did you see Miss Rose leave with her car packed?"

"Yes, Daddy, she's gone, just like I knew she would go." Bea turned around with her hands on her hips and ran back into the house.

But Sam had seen the tears gathering in his oldest daughters eyes. How could he have allowed this to happen to his daughters again?

"Odelia! Odelia, where are you?" Sam bellowed.

"I'm right here. Stop your yelling. What in the world is going on?" Odelia walked into the parlor wiping her hand on her apron.

"Did you know your niece skipped out on us?" Sam could feel the vein in his neck pulsing. "How dare she take advantage of us like this? I know you love her Odelia but there is no excuse for her to up and leave. "

"Now you wait just a minute, young man. Before you go accusing and saying things you will be sorry for later, come into the kitchen and sit down. I'll tell you over a glass of tea. I've got *etouffee* cooking on the stove, and I don't want it to burn."

Sam didn't want to hurt Odelia, but she needed to know how he felt. "I will not tolerate Rose's behavior."

"Now, Sam, I know what a hot head you can be. Drink some of this tea and cool off. Rose didn't desert us. She missed a deadline on her new book. We've all kept her so busy she needed to get away somewhere and have uninterrupted work time. So she went to Lafayette for a couple of days. She plans to return by Sunday." Odelia popped him on the arm with her dishtowel.

"Now don't you feel foolish?"

Sam calmed his shaking voice. "She still should have told the girls. Lizzy and Bea both are very upset. They think they did something wrong. You, above all people, know how long it took for them to find any happiness when Lisa left. I don't think they could handle another disappointment. She should have told them. She should have told me."

He did feel a little foolish. But the look on both the girls' faces reminded him that he would have to keep a watch on how close they got to Rose and he wouldn't allowed himself to get too attached.

"Well she better be back before Monday, I can't handle another troubled week."

"Ah, *bebé*, you worry too much. Lizzy and Bea are well loved and they know it." She went around the table and put her arm around Sam's shoulders. "Always the worrier, my little man, ever since you were a little boy. Always trying to make things right. Keep people happy."

Odelia gave Sam a squeeze and spoke in a gentle voice. "Relax a little, Sam. You don't have to do this alone. We are all here to help you raise those two beautiful girls."

"I know. I don't want to see them hurt again. That's all. I won't allow it to happen again."

"People get hurt. That's part of life. Just focus on the happy times." Something boiled over on the stove. "Now get out of here before I have to start dinner all over again." She planted a big loud kiss on his cheek. The kind she used on him when he was a small boy.

Smiling, Sam left the warmth of the kitchen in search of his daughters.

"I think she told a great big lie to Odelia. I don't think she is coming back at all." Bea put her hands back on her hips and stuck her nose a little higher in the air.

"She is too. Papa said. And 'sides Rose don't lie." Lizzy exclaimed.

"I bet you a million dollars, she's not coming back."

"Bea, that's enough. You both know if Odelia says something then it's true. Now, tomorrow I've asked Trudy to come and spend some time with you two. Try not to make it hard on her. She's doing this as a big favor." Sam tweaked Bea's nose, which caused her to lower it some. "I've got to go back to work. You girls try to stay out of mischief today and I'll see you at supper."

He might have talked Lizzy and Bea into believing that Rose was coming back, but he would have to see it to believe it. But it didn't matter to him one-way or the other. He just didn't want Odelia or the girls hurt. She could never come back as he was concerned.

"Hey, little brother. What's that mad as hell look on your face? Someone eat the last piece of Odelia's fried chicken?" Preston teased.

"No. That fool hearted woman, Rose, left this morning. It upset the girls, and as usual when it concerns a woman, I was left picking up the pieces."

"Whew. She's gone for good? I didn't pick her to be the type to up and leave like that." Preston removed his hat and wiped his forehead with his bandana. "Without telling us all good-bye."

"Odelia thinks she'll be back by Sunday, but I have my doubts. I don't care one way or the other."

Rusty stepped out from behind the combine and rolled his eyes. "Yeah, right."

Preston and Rusty shared a loud laugh as Sam stormed off to his truck and grabbed his thermos and drank some cold water.

"Okay, if you two clowns are through being stupid, we have work to do." Sam took his cap off and poured some water on his head and ran his hand through his hair. "You don't know what you're talking about."

"She has you squirming, Sam. Whether you admit it or not."

"Shut up, Rusty. I can still whip your butt and don't you forget it. I don't want to waste any more time on that redhead." Sam pulled himself up on the seat of the combine and cranked the motor. No one could tell him superstitions didn't come true. Look at the trouble she'd brought in a little over a week, and she was such a little bit of a woman.

As Trudy had promised she came and she and the girls looked like they were headed out to crab. "Hey, Sam. Want to come with us?" Trudy yelled.

Sam cut the motor and looked into the wishful eyes of his daughters. "I can't, girls. But after harvest, I promise we'll do whatever you want."

"Okay, Papa, see you later gator." Lizzy yelled over her shoulder as she skipped in front of Bea and Trudy.

"Trudy, thank you. You're a good friend. I'll repay you somehow, okay," said Sam.

"What are friends for if not to help? See you later. Maybe we'll catch enough for a big crab stew."

Sam watched as the three of them laughed and walked toward the canal. Why hadn't he felt something more for Trudy when he'd had the chance? But it was never more than friendship. Of course, he had felt what he thought was love or something for Lisa and look where it got him. Maybe a good woman, one he could please, was more what he needed? He had witnessed the love between his Mom and Dad and between Lewis and Susan. But he knew they all felt something for each other, and he would not settle for anything less. Without love and passion, he knew he would shrivel up and die inside.

CHAPTER FOUR

When Rose returned to the house. The stars were high in the sky. Clouds washed over them, blurring their twinkle. Weary from trying to force romance between her hero and her heroine in her book, she headed for the stairs. The sound of laughter coming from the living room stopped her. She sat the laptop and suitcase on the stairs and turned to the happy sounds coming from behind the slightly closed door.

Peeking inside she saw Bea, Lizzy, Trudy, Preston, and Sam playing a board game, all sitting on the floor.

"Papa, you missed the answer. You have to go back to start," Lizzy said.

"No, I don't. I didn't hear the question right. Give me another chance."

"Oh, no you don't, big brother. Lizzy's right. You have to go back to the start. You can't talk your way out of this one." Preston slapped Sam on the back and the laughter started again.

Rose stood hidden in her concealed place behind the door. Moving over to get a better view, she caught Sam staring at her. Quickly she moved away, retrieved her bags and hurried up the stairs. In the safety of her room, she flopped in the chair by the window.

She was scared. The editor wasn't too happy with her, but had extended the deadline a month. Which pushed back her release date. This book could make or break her writing career. Her readership had just climbed with the last book and she couldn't lose that momentum. This is what she did. This was who she was. She should be able to write here, especially here with all this beauty and space around her. Maybe when the harvest was over, she could find herself a little niche and write the day away. She sure wouldn't go back to Atlanta. Ever.

Fatigue overtook her and she laid her head back and closed her eyes. How nice it would be to have someone she could lean on. Just once not have to make these decisions on her own.

She had to get a grip. A long time ago she'd made up her mind that if anything good were to happen for her, she would have to be the one who made it happen. But not always alone.

A knock on the door forced her from a slouching position to a sitting one.

"Come in," she said in a weak voice.

Clearing her throat she repeated herself. "Please come in."

Sam sauntered in and hovered over her.

"Sit, please."

He continued to stand.

"You're making me nervous, Sam, please."

Sam sat in the chair on the other side of the small table between them. His eyes never left hers.

"I have something to say, Rose. I know that your intentions were good, but we have to set some rules. I can't have my daughters upset and wondering if they did something wrong every time you take a wild hair to up and leave. I won't stand back and watch their small worlds crumble believing they did something wrong."

Sam pulled himself out of the chair and began to pace. He ran his hand through his hair.

A gesture that Rose had come to recognize as a sign of frustration. A sigh escaped her lips.

"I don't understand, Sam, why are you so mad at me?"

"Why? Why, am I mad? You have got to be kidding right? You up and leave for three days and don't bother to tell the girls, or me, and you have to ask why I'm mad? By the way I'm not mad, I'm concerned. The girls thought you were gone for good." He lowered his voice and muttered, "So did I."

Rose didn't understand. His eyes turned a dark gray. Was he really concerned or extremely mad? She thought it was most likely the latter. She knew mad when she saw mad it was something she'd recognized all too often. Well, he didn't own her. He could strut around like a bantam rooster and boss everyone else, but he was not her boss.

Her eyes burned with unshed tears. She jumped from the chair and turned her back to Sam. Rose would not give him the pleasure of seeing her cry. If she could help it, no man would ever have that pleasure again.

Rose clenched her hands at her side her nails biting into her palms. Gaining control.

"I will keep our agreement, unless you want me to leave and maybe that is what I should do. You haven't wanted me here from the beginning."

"Don't even lay that on me, Rose. I never gave you any indications that I didn't want you in my home." A low growl slipped out of his mouth. "Why do women always do that? All of you have a way of turning things around so it becomes other people's faults. You don't fight fair. The facts are, you agreed to help your Aunt and watch my girls and you left without telling me. I know you told Odelia, but I was the one that should have been informed."

Rose turned her back and walked over to the window.

"Don't turn your back on me, Lisa."

Rose swung around. Sam's expression of horror and hurt blanketed his face.

"I'm not Lisa, Sam. I'll leave first thing in the morning. Give me enough time to talk to Aunt Odelia."

Sam hastened to her side in two long steps. He reached for her but drew back letting his arms fall empty at his side. In a low, slow voice he said. "You don't have to go, Rose. Lizzy and Bea are just getting used to you. And Odelia would be heart broken." He stuffed his hands in his pocket. "I—." Sam drew in a deep breath. "After the harvest if you need to leave, I'll understand. I do need you to keep me informed if you feel the urge or need to leave again so I can protect Bea and Lizzy." He let out a pent up sigh, "please."

Rose searched his face. Could anyone read this man? Did anyone know what went on in that head of his? And especially in his heart?

"All right, Sam, I'll stay for awhile, and I'll keep you informed. I, too, keep my promises Sam."

Rose held out her hand. "Agreed?"

Sam's hand grasped hers and held it tight. It wasn't a handshake, but more like he needed to hold her in place.

"Agreed," Sam said.

Eyes locked, hands held, had they both stopped breathing?

"Mind if I interrupt?" Trudy stood in the door they had forgotten to close.

Had everyone heard her discussion? Rose hoped not. Sam let go of Rose's hand.

Tearing his eyes from Rose he ambled over to the French door. "Is that rain I hear?"

"Yeah, it's been pouring for almost an hour. Didn't you hear it?" Trudy smiled a wicked smile. "Maybe not, guess you were too busy."

"It's too late for you to drive home tonight. And that rain sounds like an all-nighter. Your room is always ready, and thank you for coming to my rescue once again, Trudy. Goodnight, ladies. I need to tuck my girls in and turn in myself. This has been a very long day. I'm beat."

"Wait, I'll walk out with you Sam." Trudy tucked her arm in the crook of Sam's. "See you in the morning, Rose."

The silence in her room roared in her ears. Rose sat on her bed. What just happened? She put her head in her hands.

"Still being a disappointment to people, Rose." The little voice of her mother rang in her head.

Sam threw the covers back off the rumpled bed. How could a person be so tired and their body refuse to sleep? If he could just shut his brain down and stop reliving the episode he'd had with Rose.

Why did he always have to be in control? He knew he had overreacted, but he had to for the sake of his girls, didn't he? He paced back and forth in his room.

Not many women he knew could be trusted to keep their word. He'd done the right thing. Rose had to be put in her place. Hadn't she?

Then why did he feel so rotten? The look on her face had ripped his heart out. He knew she needed approval, he had heard Odelia talk about the little girl no one approved of for years. But Sam had lived by a code all his life and expected no less from others. One had to reap the consequences of ones actions.

Sam pulled on his jeans and walked down the hall to Lizzy and Bea's room, they had shared since Liza left. Opening the door, Sam smiled to himself. Lizzy had crawled into bed with Bea as she often did. She was pressed as close to her back as she could get.

Sam lifted his small daughter in his arms, her sweet breath blowing on his neck, and placed her gently in her own bed. Pulling the sheet over her and tucking her rag doll, Abby, in her arms, he knelt by her bed.

"I'm so sorry baby, I never wanted you to hurt, ever. I vowed to protect you and I failed. I'll be more careful next time." Sam brushed the soft curl off her face and kissed the place it had covered.

"Is anything wrong, Daddy?" Bea's sleepy voice asked.

"No, little lady. I was just moving Lizzy to her bed to give you more room. Go back to sleep," Sam whispered.

Bea closed her eyes as Sam kissed her forehead. "Night Bea. Love ya."

"Night, Daddy. Daddy, is Rose really gone?" she asked.

"No honey, she came back. She had an important business trip she had to make but she's back now. And she won't leave again, until after the harvest. She promised. Now go to sleep."

"Lizzy will be happy, but I don't think she will stay, do you?"

"I don't know, Bea, maybe if she can, she'll stay." He bent to ruffle her hair, but noticed she had fallen back to sleep. He closed the door behind him and headed back down the hall to his room.

Sam paused at Rose's door and prepared to knock, but instead leaned in and listened for a sound. There was no light coming from under the door and all was quiet, she must be asleep.

What more did he have to say anyway? As much as he didn't want to admit it, Rusty was right, she was getting under his skin, and he didn't like it. It was time for him to get his head on straight. He would have to put to rest that conversation along with his tired body.

###

In the shower, Rose let the water flow over her body until it ran cold, and dried her body dry with rough quick strokes. She pulled on a pair of shorts and tee shirt and wrapped her hair in a towel. She was bone tired but knew that sleep would escape her. Maybe she could write.

"Rose, are you awake?" Trudy's voice drifted through the closed door.

Rose opened the door to Trudy smiling as she held up two beers.

"Thought you could use a drink and a friendly face."

"Trudy, you are a mind reader. Let's take these out on the gallery I could use some fresh air." Rose slid her feet into her fuzzy pink slippers, took one of the beers from Trudy and headed out the French door.

"Don't you just love this place? I think it is the most beautiful place in the world. I wonder if the LeBlancs know how very lucky they are," Trudy said.

"It is lovely. And to make matters worse I know I have to leave soon."

Taking a big sip of the cold beer she shook her head.

Rose chuckled. "We are sure a sad lot. A single woman and a lonesome married woman sitting in the dark alone drinking and wishing in a house full of men."

"Honey, I wished for so many years, and what I got was well worth the wait. It's not perfect. I miss him so when he is gone. But I knew what he did when I met him, so there is no crying over his choice of work anymore."

The two new friends enjoyed each other's company when silence filled the air.

"Tell me, Trudy, how do you handle the loneliness? I don't mean being alone. I know the difference. Alone I can take; I've learned to live with that. But I'm terrified of loneliness."

Trudy didn't respond giving Rose the freedom to continue.

"Please don't repeat this to anyone, but that's why I don't want to leave. This is the first place I've ever not felt lonely."

"Do I ever know what you're talking about, sister? I've been around the dance floor with many a partner, but I'd never felt the music until I met my Leon. You can trust me with your secrets, Rose, and if you want to share, I'm not the least bit tired. Tell me about the men in your life, and then I'll tell you about mine."

Could she share her hurts and humiliation with Trudy? She had never had anyone to listen to her.

Rose opened her mouth and the words tumbled out so fast she could hardly take a breath.

"I've been a disappointment to men all my life. I must have been a disappointment to even my father because Mother said he left right after I was born. She told me more than once I was the ugliest baby she had ever seen. What mother thinks that? What mother thinks her little baby is ugly? No wonder my dad left. She's been trying to change me ever since."

Rose drank the rest of her beer and sat the empty bottle on the small table between the rockers. Drawing her knees up to her chin she wrapped her arms around them and rested her head.

"But then I met Billy in high school. He was shy and tender. I loved him dearly. Against my mother's wishes we became engaged, and I have no doubt, if he would have lived, we would be raising our family today. He was as close to happy endings I've ever had. But life has a way of taking care of best-laid plans. After him, no man cared enough to fight for me. Of course, none of the men were of my choosing. Mother talked me into letting her pick out the perfect man for me. She set me up with men of importance, men of influence, men like her, perfect. Men who focused on my faults."

Rose shifted in her chair.

"One after another came and went. Never really seeing me. Then came Ted. A hunk of a man, pro quarterback. Everyone loved Ted, so I thought I had to love him too. But I disappointed him so much he left me at the altar."

Rose felt Trudy touch her arm and remembered someone was listening. She'd forgotten. It felt so good to empty her heart, free her soul.

"Trudy, I'm so sorry. Here I've been going on and on about my relationships. I've monopolized the conversation and not let you get a word in. You should have stopped me earlier." Rose let out a long sigh. "I'm new to this friendship thing. Please forgive me."

"Honey, there is nothing to apologize for." Trudy stood and stretched. "You know what we need? Another beer. I thought my love life sucked, but you beat me by leaps and bounds. What you need is some good hard loving from a real man. What you've had so far is the pits."

Trudy picked up her empty and headed for the door. "Let's go see what we can find in the kitchen. Our pity party needs to move to a new level. Do you like fudge? I feel like cooking up a pot of fudge. Nothing beats chocolate for making a woman happy, even if we have to eat the whole pot."

Rose was sitting on the cabinet eating warm fudge out of a bowl with a spoon, laughing at Trudy's off color jokes when Preston and Randy stumbled into the room. Both looked as if they had just got out of bed.

"I told you I smelled fudge. Don't ever question me about my knowledge of food, little brother." Preston punched Randy's arm.

"Hey beautiful ladies, care to share with two hungry men."

"Maybe, but it might take at least three more compliments."

Preston walked over and nuzzled his head on Trudy's shoulder. "Please you beautiful, sexy thing."

"Oh, go on. Help yourself, If I eat anymore, I'll be sick all night," said Trudy.

Preston and Trudy took turns telling stories they swore were true. The four laughed, drank and ate until close to midnight.

"I could curl up on this cabinet and fall asleep. As much fun as this has been, I think I'll pull myself upstairs and go to bed." Rose stumbled as she got off the counter top. Randy caught her.

"Careful, little lady." He picked her up and grinned. "Want me to tuck you in?"

"No. Put me down. This I can do on my own. Thanks guys. You have helped turn this awful day into one of greatest I've spent." Turning to Trudy she mouthed, "thank you, my friend."

###

Around two in the morning, Rose woke with her stomach doing flips. Dashing to the bathroom, she lost the beer and fudge. For what felt like hours, she hugged the toilet. Exhausted, she crumbled into a fetal position, laying her face on the cool floor and closed her eyes.

Rose felt strong arms carrying her. Forcing her eyes to open slightly, she stared into Sam's face.

"No." She groaned. "Oh God, let this be a nightmare. Please say you haven't seen me like this. Please."

"Hush, you're not the first person I've rescued from the bathroom floor, remember I have brothers."

He laid her on the bed and covered her shaking body then turned and went back to the bathroom. He returned with a cool washcloth and wiped her face.

"How did you know I was sick?"

"You left the French doors open and I came to check if you were all right. You weren't in your bed so I went looking for you."

"I'm sorry, Sam. You should have left me to die on the bathroom floor. I don't know what happened. It felt so good going down. I guess fudge and beer don't mix. You better go check on Preston, Randy and Trudy. They ate and drank more than I did."

"Don't worry about Preston, he has an iron stomach, and Trudy and Randy can take care of themselves. Now get some rest."

"Sam, can I ask you a question? Why don't you like me? You are always so mad at me." Rose buried her head deeper into her pillow and pulled the sheet up around her ears. "If you tell me what you want, I can change, I'm good at trying to be what a man wants me to be."

"Don't be ridiculous. I don't dislike you. Now close your eyes and try to sleep this off."

"But Sam," she heard her voice fade and could hear Sam's voice whispering, what was he saying?

"You don't have to change for me, little Rose. You don't have to change for anyone. Even though you're a handful of trouble, you are great just the way you are." He gently kissed her forehead, tucked the covers around her and closed the French doors quietly behind him.

Oh if this is a dream let it continue.

Sunlight warmed Rose's face and the strong smell of magnolias forced her to open her eyes. Pain shot through her head as if it were held tight in a vise.

She opened her mouth to speak and her tongue stuck to the roof of her mouth. "Oh, God, what did I do?"

Moaning, she rose to a sitting position. Then she placed her head between her hands and took a deep breath.

"Okay, Rose, get it together, you didn't hurt anyone. Did you? No one but yourself," she muttered.

Rose walked across the floor, her feet hardly touching the cool hardwood. She had to get that taste out of her mouth. Looking in the mirror, Rose saw the reflection of a girl's face with deep dark circles under her eyes, her hair slicked to her head on the right side. Thank goodness no one had seen her in this shape.

"Sam!" Her eyes opened wider, as her mind cleared. "Oh God, Sam was here last night." It wasn't a dream. No wonder he thinks I'm such a loser. I am a loser.

Somehow she would have to make up for this. She had promised to take care of his daughters, and so far she had taken off without informing him and drank too much with Trudy and his brothers. Enough play time, it was time to buckle down and take this job and her job of writing seriously.

Rose found her aunt in the kitchen humming a song and stirring a large pot of food on the stove.

"Where is everyone? The house is so quiet." Rose said.

"Rose. How are you feeling? Sam told us you had a headache and to let you sleep. Sit let me get you some coffee and something to eat, you look like you still feel bad." Odelia poured a cup of coffee and fixed Rose some toast.

"Trudy took the girls into town to help her clean out one of her storerooms and Sam and the rest of the crew are out in the rice fields. So it's just me and you, my dear."

Odelia poured herself a cup of coffee and turned her stove off. "You know I'm pretty caught up. Did you get the work done on your book you needed to?"

"No, I thought I just needed to get away. You know, be quiet and not be disturbed? But I just couldn't focus. All I did was spend my time wondering what everyone was doing here. Every time I tried to get into my book, my mind would wander to you in your kitchen, stirring up some unbelievable dish. Or the sound that the wind makes as it rustles though those old oak trees. Or if *Tante* Ina would visit my room again like she did last night."

Rose poured another cup of coffee.

"I called my editor before I came back, and she gave me an extension. This is the first time I've had to ask for one. This book started out so good, but now, I don't know so much is missing."

"Does talking about it help? I'm a good listener. Can't help you any with the writing, but I do read and I know what I love in a book."

"I don't know Aunt Odelia, it's like I don't believe in romance any more, can you imagine?" Rose rinsed her cup and gazed out the window above the sink. It overlooked a covered patio with large pots of fresh herbs. Such a charming peaceful place, maybe she could work that into one of her scenes.

"I think it might even go deeper than not believing in romance. Maybe I don't believe in love, at least real love. Love that endures. I don't know, I'm a mess. How can I write a romance if I don't believe in love?"

Odelia put her hand over Rose's hand. "Rose, come with me, I have something to show you and a story to tell."

Rose followed Odelia to the house that had been her Aunt's home all these past years. She opened the door to walls without sheetrock in the living room. She led Rose into a bedroom shut off from the construction in the other rooms. It was painted yellow and housed a sled bed with a yellow and white nine-patch quilt. White gauzy curtains graced the windows and a small lime green comfy chair sat facing the window, placed as if someone sat waiting. From the window, one could see almost straight down the long tree lined drive way. Rose let the soft curtain fall from between her fingers as she turned from the window.

"What a lovely room, Aunt Odelia. This is yours?"

"Yes, honey child, and I sure miss being here. Sam said the builder told him I could move back in about two weeks." She opened the closet and motion to Rose. "Help me pull this trunk out of my closet will you, Hon?" she asked. With the trunk next to the bed, Odelia sat on the bed's edge. "Rose, grab that chair and sit by me while I tell you a story."

Rose pulled a wing back chair from across the room. It had wide yellow and white stripes with small green leaves scattered between the stripes. A small green velvet pillow rested where one's back would relax. This had to be her aunt's favorite chair. Or was it the small lime colored chair by the window? Rose looked at her aunt's face dotted with tired deep lines. "Aunt Odelia, I think you need this chair more than me, okay?"

"I'm fine right here." She patted the bed. "I want you to know there is nothing that is more important to me than you are, and if this helps you in any way, then it is time well spent. Now sit back, I only know one way to tell a story and that's with lots of detail, so make yourself comfortable."

Her aunt looked out the window for a while and in a low voice began her tale. "When I was a young woman I met the love of my life at the American Legion Hall in Bon Amie. When he walked through that door, he stole my breath. Each step was full of confidence. He was tall and so very handsome. He scanned the room and when his eyes caught mine, I thought my heart would beat right out of my chest. That tall good-looking man walked right across that dance floor, sauntered up to me with his hand outstretched. 'I believe this is our dance,' he said, a charming grin on his face. We danced every dance together and after that night saw each other every chance we could get. It was a true whirlwind romance."

Odelia let out a deep sigh. "Wilson never proposed officially. We both just knew one day we would be married. We even set the date once, an early spring ceremony was planned. Then the draft notice came in the mail. Wilson was to report for training and then active duty."

A heavy sigh, almost a gasp caught her aunt's breath.

"Aunt Odelia if this is uncomfortable for you I can hear this story another time."

"No, Rose, I feel you need to hear it now, and I need to tell it."

She reached over and squeezed Rose's hand.

"Wilson and I decided that we would wait until his first furlough and get married then. After all the Vietnam war was not supposed to last very long. What were the chances he would see any action?"

"Wilson told me not to worry, that our love was strong enough to last. When I cried he took me in his warm arms and whispered that he would love me until it snowed on the magnolias. Tears turned to laughter at that impossibility, and then we kissed each other in confirmation. The day he pulled out of town, I'll never forget how he looked in his uniform. So brave, a tender smile on his lips as tears ran down his face. He handed me a magnolia and kissed me good-bye. I promised I would write him a letter every Sunday until he came home to me. He agreed to do the same. Then he was gone."

Odelia wiped the tears now flowing silently down her soft full cheeks.

"I only received a few letters from Wilson before he shipped out to Vietnam. I received two more from a small village in Vietnam I couldn't even pronounce. Then the letters stopped. Some of my letters came back unopened. Others disappeared. I continued to write every Sunday hoping one would get to him, praying he was alive to receive them. I finally stopped sending them."

"Did you ever find out what happened to him?"

"I tried for years, but I didn't have the resources or the knowledge to do much. The army was very closed mouthed about any information concerning him. They couldn't or wouldn't tell me if he was dead or alive. Over the years, the hurt and longing faded, but the love I felt for him is just as strong today as yesterday, if not stronger. And deep down, I know he still loves me too. After all, it hasn't snowed on the magnolias, yet."

Odelia reached over and raised the lid on the large trunk reveling a trunk full of memories all hand written.

Rose was on her knees before she knew it looking at the many, many objects of love.

Odelia reached for a group of letters and handed them to Rose.

As Rose began to read the name and date written on the front of the envelopes, some yellowed with age, she realized her hands were shaking. "I thought you said you'd stopped writing him."

"No, I said I stopped mailing them. I made a promise. So every Sunday I write a letter to Wilson. I've done this for so long that now it's a part of my life. I tell Wilson everything. I share my laughter and disappointments with him. It keeps him alive in my heart." Odelia put her head down, I know you will think I'm crazy, but sometimes I feel those strong arms wrapped around me, and in this room he leads me across the floor in a waltz."

She handed Rose more letters. "You are welcome to read them, my dear. I don't have anything to hide or anything to be ashamed of. That's what love is you know. I wanted you to know there is true love in this world. Lasting love. It is a precious thing and you have to be very careful when you find it and hold it tight. Hold it tight and never let it die. And it doesn't matter if you are both together or not, the love is always still there."

"I don't know what to say, Aunt Odelia. I didn't know. I am so selfish. Always whining about my troubles. I love you so much." Rose said as she hugged her aunt.

"I'll send one of the boys over to move this trunk to your bedroom. You can go through them at your leisure. Maybe when you read through a few of them, you will believe in love. Then maybe you can finish your book." She paused in her steps and sighed. "Boy, I'm tired, this took more out of me than I thought. I think I'll lie down for a little while. Why don't you walk me back to the Big house, will you love?"

"Aunt Odelia, thank you for sharing this with me. I'll be very careful with your memories. And don't worry about anything, I'm sure I can finish whatever you have on the stove."

"Oh you don't have to worry about dinner. I only need a power nap. The meal is cooked; it will just need to be re-heated when it's dinner

CHAPTER FIVE

Rose spent the rest of the afternoon trying to sort the letters by date. She read the first letters as two lovers shared their longing and love for each other. Then when Wilson shipped out to Vietnam, his letters changed and he wrote of unspoken horrors in the war-strewn villages. He wrote about his fears and sorrow for the innocent people that always have to suffer in wartime. But he always ended his letters about his complete love for Odelia and their future together.

The letters made Rose laugh and sometimes cry. Through all the words, the love between the two young people came shining through. She lay back on the floor among the hundreds of letters and closed her eyes. To have a love such as theirs was a once in a lifetime gift.

Rose awoke from a dream filled with soldiers dressed in full uniform. Her soldier wore blue and when he turned around Sam's face smiled at her.

"Stupid, crazy dream."

"Talking to yourself, Rose?"

Sam leaned against the doorframe with one of his hands in his jean pocket. He held his cap in his other hand, leaving his dark black hair in a mess of curls. He looked more handsome in those jeans than he could ever look in anything else. They fit him. Told who he was. A man with a little starch to keep him straight and strong, a few patches to cover his hurts and a tight fit to show a man comfortable in his own skin. Did he ever relax or was he just all work? One thing for sure, he gave the impression of being in control of his world.

"What is all this?" he asked as he entered her room.

"Odelia's letters. Did you know about this?" Rose stood and handed a few to Sam.

"Whoa, these are her letters to Wilson? She talked about him a lot when I was a young boy. But she hasn't talked about him in a long while. I remember that we were not allowed to bother her when she was writing her letters." He turned one of the envelopes over and looked at the current date. "I didn't know she still wrote to him."

"Every Sunday." Rose shook her head. "I wonder why no one ever found him?"

"I guess he didn't want to be found or he is dead." He handed the letters back to Rose. "Are you busy?"

"No. This can wait. Do you need me to do something with the girls?"

"No, they're still with Trudy. Odelia and Preston went to get them and stop by the store. You mentioned you wanted a tour of the place and this is as good a time as any."

"I'll get my shoes. Are you sure this won't interfere with your work?"

"I wouldn't offer if I didn't have the time. We'll start upstairs. "There are eight bedrooms on this floor, four that face the back and four that face the front. The four in the front were added about 1926 when the upstairs ballroom was converted. This is the original staircase and was all hand carved." Sam led the way down stairs, his voice confident with each word filled with pride as he described his home.

"How old is this place?"

"Eighteen hundred acres were part of a 1796 Spanish land grant. My ancestors bought the land in 1800. The houses were started soon after. The lower floor was built *poteaux sur solle* style, where the house is put on cypress blocks about two feet off the ground. This helps with flooding problems and also with cooling in the summer months, even insect control. The walls are cypress studs and packed with a mixture of clay and Spanish moss called *bousillage*, which has proved to be a very good insulation." Sam looked down at Rose. "Are you bored yet?"

"No, please go on." Rose answered.

"All the materials to build this place came off our land. The cypress and cedar came from the swamp land on our property and was processed at our sawmill."

Sam stopped and touched Rose's elbow. "See that window in the hallway? Looks out of place don't it? But if you notice it lines up with one on either side of the outside of the house. That's so nothing blocks the cross venation. They thought of everything back then, you know?" A smile lingered on his lips as he drifted back in time. "I still like to open the windows in the fall and let the air come through. Sometimes I can hear one of my grandparents saying, good job, Sam."

Rose felt his hand warm on her skin. The passion in his voice caused her breath to catch. Had she ever been part of anything in her life that made her feel that passionate? After a moment she let breath out. Maybe her writing.

"Are you okay? Are you sure I'm not boring you?"

"I'm fine. I find this fascinating. Please continue."

Sam led her to his office where she had seen the large portrait over the fireplace.

"These are the five that started the whole thing. The man on the left is

Percy LeBlanc and his wife, Agnes; the woman in the middle is the *vielle fille*, old maid, of the family, Ina." Sam turned and looked down at Rose, "It is told that she had a lot of fire for such a small woman." He stared back at the portrait. "You can tell she was a real spitfire. I wished I'd met her." Sam continued. "The last two are Gray LeBlanc, and his wife Charlotte. They are the two that built the Gray house. Charlotte didn't believe in two story houses, said when she looked out the window she wanted to see the ground not the tree tops, so her home was all on one level."

Rose couldn't help but keep her attention on Sam's face as he peered at his relatives with such respect. He truly loved every bit of the history of this place.

"You know, Rose, I truly feel like I knew each and every one of them. The stories these people could tell. They endured much, so we could enjoy all of this," he said as he swept his hand in the air to encompass the room.

Rose stood on her tiptoes to get up as close to the painting as she could and took a second look. "Wait a minute. Ina? Isn't that the name of your ghost? Is that her? And why the smell of magnolias?" Rose glared at the tiny woman with the mischievous face and impish grin in the portrait.

"That's her. I told you she was harmless, unless you cross her. I think the two of you are about the same size. The scent is from the blooms she always carried in her apron pockets. They come from a Banana Magnolia tree. The only ones we have on the property now are way on the other side of Lewis's house. But one of the journals states that a big Banana Magnolia tree grew outside one of the bedroom windows. I like to think it was her bedroom." A large grin slid into place on his face. "Make a believer out of you yet?"

"I'm not sure. The smell is so strong at times. I don't know what I believe anymore."

Sam continued to show Rose around the house and they ended up in the kitchen. "Wait, did Odelia show you this?" He pointed to a small door in the middle of a wall that had been hidden by a large tapestry he moved aside.

"No she didn't. What is it?"

"It's a kind of dumb waiter. That in itself is amazing, but it's the story surrounded it that is the most interesting. The family that lived here during the Civil War used it to hide in until the Union soldiers were gone and they could escape. They stayed hidden three days without food or water. My great-great grandfather was seven at the time."

Rose moved up to get a better look at the place of hiding when she stumbled on a rug and started to fall.

Sam's strong arms stopped her from hitting her head. He held her against his chest. So tightly she could hardly breathe, but she dared not move. If she did it would break the spell. And right now it felt good, real good, too right to be let go. She inhaled. Fresh pine, or was it cedar? His chest was solid like his arms. Strong enough to protect the people he loved. She could hear the beating of his heart as it quickened and became louder. Rose closed her eyes. What would it be like to have someone to always be there to catch you when you fell?

"Are you okay, Rose?"

"Yes," she whispered. Expecting him to let her go he still held her close.

His breath evened out before he released his hold on her. "You need to be careful."

Rose straightened her shirt and broke eye contact with Sam. Yes, indeed she would have to be very careful.

"I need to get back to work. That concludes the two-bit tour. When I have more time, I'll show you more. If you have any questions let me know." He started out of the room but turned back. "If you're interested, we have some old journals in my office you could read. I would rather you didn't remove them, they are important to our family."

"Thanks, Sam. You don't know how much this has helped. Now if you will excuse me, I want to write some of this information down." Rose bounded up the steps. Not sure if she was running to her work or away from Sam.

Sam wiped the sweat off his face and was met with her scent still on his hands. He could still feel the softness of her skin and the frailness of her body as it was pressed against his. And those damn green eyes. They would have to be the color of new spring. Eyes always searching for approval. He couldn't shake them from his mind. All he thought about was protecting her.

Rose made a man want to make her happy and keep her safe. But it was very clear to him that he was not that man. He could not take those chances, not with his daughters. Not with the welfare of all of his family. He would not. He just needed to keep his distance, and for goodness sake avoid being alone with her. He had to get back to work.

"Lewis, where are Preston, Randy and Rusty. The plan was to check out the bins this afternoon. If they've gone off somewhere, I swear."

"Hold on, Sam. What's got you on the warpath? Rusty and Randy have gone into town to get some parts for the combine. We've checked out all the bins except this one, so settle down."

Sam spat on the ground. Trying to remove the nasty taste of guilt from his mouth. His shortcomings were not his brother's fault. He was just the closest one for Sam to unload his rant. "Sorry, Lewis. It's that damn woman."

Lewis wiped his greasy hands on the red cloth hanging from his jeans. "What's got you so worked up? What damn woman? Rose?"

"Yes. Who else, Rose? I knew she would be trouble, with her red hair and green eyes."

"What did she do this time? Run away again?"

Sam pretended to check out the door to the bin.

"No. She's just so, needy. I don't know, Lewis. She just rubs me the wrong way. You know."

A large grin spread across Lewis's face. "Yeah, I do know, little brother."

Sam caught the grin on his brother's face before Lewis could wipe it away. "Now don't start getting ideas. I knew I shouldn't have said anything to you." Sam walked around to the other side of the bin. "I'll be glad when this season is over and my life returns to normal. Whatever normal is."

"Slow down a minute, Sam. Maybe this is normal, if you have feelings for this woman, then what is more normal than that?"

"I never said I had feelings for Rose. Don't be putting words in my mouth." Sam removed his cap and ran his hand over his head. "I don't need another woman in my life. I can take care of things myself."

"Can you? Maybe it's time you stop licking your wounds and some thoughts together about what your girls might need, little brother."

Sam's tense muscles in his jaw hardened to stone as he looked at his oldest brother, his voice shook as he spoke. "Shut up, Lewis, you don't know what you're talking about. The girls is what's always on my mind, the first thing in the morning and the last thing to cross my mind and heart at night. So don't even try to pretend you know what worries me on a daily basis or how I feel about anyone." He pulled his cap on his head and balled his hands into a fist.

"What you going to do, hit me? Just hear me out and I won't say another word."

Sam was breathing hard. He had gotten mad at his brothers before, but this time was different, and he didn't even know why. Sometimes he was easy to anger but always quick to get over it, but not this time.

"Go ahead, say your piece. Then never give me advice about what I need again." Sam relaxed his hands.

Lewis lowered his voice.

"Sam, all I want to say is consider what your daughters are missing. Sure they get a lot of love from all of us. And Odelia is great with them. But think back, Sam. We grew up without a mother, and it's hard. Damn hard. They give a child something no one else can. Especially, for little girls. They need someone to fuss over their hair, wipe away their tears and give them advice about boys. They will soon ask questions that only another female can answer, if they haven't already."

"That woman is not Rose. She is not the motherly type. Thank you for being concerned. But I can do all those things myself. You remember how it was when Lisa left. I will not be left to put Lizzy's and Bea's world back together again."

"Not all women are like Lisa."

"I know that. But in all honesty, you scooped up one of the last good ones. And frankly, I don't have the energy or the leisure to sort them out. This one's good, this one's bad, this one might work. No thank you, what a nightmare that would be. Sam turned to leave. "I'm going to check the fields. See you at supper."

Lewis was right about one thing. It was hard growing up without a mother. Was he being selfish? Sam shook his head, and walked a little faster, trying to outrun his thoughts. No, his instinct was right. He'd been down that road and he could not, no, he would not, chance love for another woman again.

Rose spent the rest of the afternoon hunched over her laptop. Fingers flew as the words flowed. A soft knock stopped her concentration.

"Odelia said to tell you that dinner would be ready in about thirty minutes," Bea said as she peeked around Rose to the mess of letters on the floor. Lizzy came running up behind her and almost bumped into her.

"You made a big mess, Rose." Lizzy walked around Bea and came and stood in the middle of the letters. "Did you write all these letters?"

Rose sat on the floor and started gathering the letters into small stacks in the top of the trunk. "These are Aunt Odelia's private letters to a soldier she once knew. Do you two want to help me pick them up and stack them nicely?"

Bea sat on the floor next to Rose and picked up an open letter. "Are these goofy love letters or something?"

"You could say that they are love letters, but I would not classify them as goofy. They are very important to her, and it would make her sad if we tore one or misplaced one. See if you can stack them in the piles I started. They are by date order. May 1980, over here and June here. Understand?"

"Yes, I understand. I can read you know." Bea gave Rose a frustrated look.

Rose chose to ignore Bea's sour disposition. "Lizzy why don't you place them neatly in the trunk when we hand them to you?"

"Okay." Lizzy knelt on the floor and smiled up at Rose. "Tell us one of your stories, Miss Rose."

"My stories are for grown-ups." When she looked at Lizzy's disappointed face she added, "But I could tell you one about a doll. A very special doll, if you like."

"Yes, yes, please do," Lizzy begged. Bea rolled her eyes.

As they worked Rose told the story that played out in her head.

"Once there was a little girl, much your size Lizzy, who moved to a new house with her parents. They moved from a small house in a large city to a very large house way back in the country a long way to a small town. The little girl was lonely. They didn't have neighbors for miles around. She was very sad. One day her grandmother came to visit. She brought the little girl a present. When she opened the box she found a beautiful doll, just like your Miss Abby, Lizzy. But this doll could do magic. She could grant any wish the little girl might ask. The first thing she asked for was a big sister to share all her dreams with. And, poof, she had a big sister who looks a lot like Bea when she smiles. And the magical thing about that wish was that the little girl was never lonely again. And the two sisters' wishes all came true."

Bea huffed and looked up at Rose. "Did you read that somewhere or what?" she asked.

"No, I made it up. Like I do my books. Did you like it?"

"In your head? You just made that story up in your head?" Bea shook her head in disbelief.

"No, Bea. Didn't you hear the story? She got it out of her heart. The story is about you, isn't it Rose? Because all wishes come true in your heart, right?"

Lizzy put her small arm around Rose's shoulders.

"You're a smart little girl, Lizzy. I guess some of that story was about me. But all my wishes have not come true. But I keep wishing. Well that's the last of the letters. Thank you both so much for helping me. Why don't you go wash up for dinner, and I will join you soon."

How could such a little person understand something Rose had tried to understand for years? She had looked for something magic to make her dreams come true, but the only magic she'd found came from her own making. Somewhere along the way she had stopped believing in magic. Maybe it was time to believe again, she thought as she placed the last letter she was holding in the trunk. Romance could start with Odelia's letters.

Bea and Lizzy came to Rose's room every afternoon to help her. Rose had talked to Sam and picked Bea up some books at the library. They included some of the classics that she'd read over and over when she was Bea's age.

"If you really want to be a writer one day, Bea, this is the first step, read, read and read some more. When you finish those, we can go to a book store in the nearest city and buy some you pick out yourself."

Bea grunted a thank you. But Rose saw the interest in her eyes. She even caught Bea smiling every now and then as she read.

Rose had picked up a couple of drawing books and told Lizzy she could be an illustrator. Lizzy would lay on her stomach on the floor, her little tongue working so hard as her little fingers drew one picture after another.

While the girls drew and read, Rose looked up web sites with information on missing persons. Somehow she was driven to help her aunt with her dream. Mostly she came up against a dead end. Wilson James proved to be a very popular name. Could she find out what had happen to him? Could she help make Aunt Odelia's dreams come true? Or did the truth lie in what Sam said. Maybe Wilson didn't want to be found. Or maybe he was dead. No matter. She didn't have to tell anyone what she found out until she knew if the news would do more harm than good. Her aunt should know. She needed to know.

CHAPTER SIX

"Hey Sam, when I was in town this morning Mr. Chesson told me that a cousin of Fred Poole has a nearly new combine he's willing to sell at a great price. He plans to take it to an auction in Mississippi this weekend. If you want to look at it, I have his phone number," Randy said.

"Man, that could be the answer we were trying to settle on brother." Lewis pointed his fork at Sam. "The money it will take to fix the number two combine is going to be a lot, and then it's so old we're not sure it will hold. I'd go, but I don't really want to leave Susan."

"I'll see what Preston has planned for this weekend when he gets in from the field." Sam stood and stretched. "Where is everyone this morning?

"Odelia and the girls left early this morning, something about making some sort of surprise for Susan." Lewis grinned. "If you are asking about Rose, she met me on the path to visit Susan this morning. Susan sure likes that little lady. In fact, she's a likeable person, don't you think, little brother? And she's not hard on the eyes either."

Sam saw the twinkle in Lewis's eyes. "Don't start with me Lewis. Come on we have work to do."

"Rose I'm so happy to see you and we have a couple of hours to ourselves. What's that in your hand?"

Susan sat in her chaise wearing a pale blue lounge dress. Rose's heart filled at how her new friend's eyes lit up with excitement to have company. She and Susan had hit it off the first time they met; she was so easy to talk to.

Maybe this was what it felt like to have a sister.

Rose relaxed in the chair next to Susan then removed her shoes and curled her feet under her. "I'm sorry I haven't been able to visit in a couple of days, but my new book is so much fun. The pages are just flying, and I didn't want to stop the flow."

"Oh, that's great, I can't wait to read it. I so enjoyed the last book. You are very talented, Rose. The characters seem to walk off the page, and I find myself thinking about them long after I finish the book. I hope you know how talented you are. I could never do what you do."

"That means a lot to me, no one but my editor and some of my readers have told me I was talented." Rose swallowed the lump in her throat and remembered the letter of her aunt she had permission to show Susan.

"My story took off with the help of Aunt Odelia and her love story. Have you ever heard it?"

"No." Susan sat up a little taller, put her hand on her chest and almost squealed with delight. "Our Odelia? Has a love story? Please share and don't you dare leave out any details."

Rose recited the story and ended with the love letters. "I brought you one to read. Aunt Odelia said it was okay. Oh, Susan, the letters are all so lovely. I feel that I have known these two people all their lives. They had such strong love for each other."

As Susan read the letter silent tears glided down her cheeks and raw emotions flooded her face. "Odelia never heard from him? Never heard if he is alive or dead? How very sad, but she's kept the faith and has kept her promise."

"I get so sad when I think of her not knowing. She has a little lime colored chair that sits in front of the window in her bedroom. It faces the outside, and the thought of her sitting and watching and waiting breaks my heart." Rose sighed.

"There's more that I have to tell you Susan." Rose felt her heart quicken as she sat on the edge of her chair. "I think I've found him. I won't know, of course, until I talk to him, but I really think it's him. Same age, same military background, and the best part, he's not that far away."

"You mean Wilson? You think you have found Wilson? What does Odelia say?"

"Oh, she doesn't know I found him. She doesn't even know I've been looking for him. No one knows. I don't want to tell her until I know for sure; I don't want to give her false hope. This might be the wrong Wilson." Rose wrapped her arms around her body, she wanted to find this man more than she'd wanted anything in a long while. "I have to somehow get Sam to let me go away this weekend, and after he got mad at me for last weekend, I have to plan my next move carefully."

Rose walked to the drop leaf tea wagon and poured them each a cup of tea, picked up a couple of cookies that Odelia had sent to Susan and took the letter back. "What do you think? Am I being foolish? I don't want to open a can of worms and cause anyone pain."

"Honey, if you were Odelia, would you want to know? No matter what the answer is? I would. The thought of not knowing if Lewis was alive or dead, happy or unhappy, would cause me a slow death." Susan patted her round stomach. "If it wasn't for this little one, I would be right there with you. Do you think he's married with a dozen kids? Or do you think he just fell out of love with Odelia?"

"I don't think a love like theirs would ever die. But who am I to say, with my track record?" Rose covered her heart with her hand, "I think if I had someone that loved me like that I would be very much like Aunt Odelia and sit in my chair by the window and pray he would walk back into my life."

Susan put her head down for a moment. "You know, Rose, I think something happened to Wilson that he didn't want to burden Odelia with. You know men. The macho in them, in his man-mind he probably thought it would be best for her if she not know. Men. Don't they know that a woman that devoted will pine for him for as long as she lives? So even if he is married with a dozen kids, I think Odelia still needs to know."

Rose and Susan's chat ended when two boisterous voices filtered in from the porch and spilled into the hallway.

"Did you see how fast that heifer hauled ass to the pasture when that rooster got after her? Man that chicken thought he was as big as an ostrich, he certainly was all feathered up. I haven't laughed that hard in I don't know when."

"Wonder what that heifer did to upset him so?" One could tell from the sound that Lewis's laughter started deep in his boots and traveled all the way up his body.

"Who knows, maybe she just looked at him wrong. Man that felt good." Sam motioned to Lewis with his finger to his lips. "We better keep it down, Susan might be resting." Susan's voice traveled down the hall. "Who could rest with all that noise? Besides I have very important company. Come and join us."

Lewis walked up to his wife, hat in hand and a gleam in his eyes. "Hey beautiful, how you feel?"

Rose knew she should look away and give them privacy, but the sweetness of the way they gazed at each other drew her in. She had to hold back a sigh when Lewis gave Susan the lightest of kisses all over her face.

"Okay you two, can't that wait until we leave?"

Rose jerked her head around to see Sam standing behind her. She was so involved with Lewis and Susan that she didn't hear him come in.

"Hi, Red. I didn't know you were coming here today. Hey little momma, how are you feeling today?"

"I'm feeling just fine. A little tired but I always am this time of the day. This little one has sure been active this morning. Rose come here, feel this." Susan placed Rose's hand on her moving stomach.

"Mercy, is it okay for him to move that much? This is so unbelievable, a baby, alive and moving, in such a small area. Does it hurt?"

Laughter came easy to Susan. "No, it doesn't hurt. I love every minute of that movement, and I can't wait until he's born so I can watch him and see what he's been doing in there. You know chin-ups, boxing or just turning flips. I think just now he was seeing how far he could stretch his arms out." Susan stifled a yawn.

"Come on, Rose I'll walk you to the house. Susan needs her rest. See you later, Lewis." Sam slapped his brother on the back and Lewis grunted as if Sam had delivered a powerful blow.

"Bye Susan, we'll talk again tomorrow. I'll let you know more about what I find. Thank you for listening." Rose kissed Susan's forehead and clutched the letter in her hand.

The day was beautiful, crisp, and clear with a slight breeze blowing. Rose had hurried alone the same path earlier that morning with a mission of sharing her plans with Susan. But now, walking beside Sam, she was able to relax and notice the beauty around her.

"Sam, do you have any idea how beautiful this place really is? You and your family are so lucky, I hope you are able to keep it the same forever, a place this beautiful needs to be enjoyed."

Sam stopped under the shade of a grand oak. His hands tucked in his back jean pockets gave him the appearance of the young boy she once knew.

"Is something wrong?"

"You really like this place?"

"Who wouldn't? It's so grand, a place you would see in the movies. And to think your family built all this. Someone cared enough throughout the years to preserve it for future generations." Rose found herself beside Sam. She gazed at her surroundings as they stood beside each other, afraid to breath, afraid to break the spell.

"It's like your family never dies. Their souls and hearts just take on new faces. As I said before, who wouldn't love this place?"

Sam cleared his throat as he now turned his attention to Rose. "Lisa, hated *Annees Passees*. She said it smothered her. The trees, the old furniture, and of course the family. She hated the lack of privacy, someone always around. That's what she kept saying she hated the most."

Rose didn't want to blink. Afraid he would stop talking. She'd wanted to know why Lisa left a perfect life, and now Sam trusted her enough to tell.

Sam sat on a log at Rose's feet. "She begged me to move. 'You can get a job in the city doing something,' she said more than once. I thought by building her a special place in the house she would forget the city. I had that empty sunroom added on, but she wouldn't even go inside, never had the desire to even decorate the room. I offered to take her to the city once a month for a weekend, we went one weekend, but after I wouldn't look at houses to buy with her, we never went again." Sam picked up a stick and drew in the dirt. "She knew that this place was a part of me and that I couldn't ever leave, but she didn't care."

Rose sat beside him. She longed to touch his arm, she felt his hurt and frustration. God, she'd had the lack of ability to please all her life. Somehow it made her disappointments easier knowing someone like Sam had the same problems.

"After Lizzy was born, Lisa withdrew more. The baby's cries irritated her, so I got up with Lizzy at night. I knew Lisa was in a deep depression, so I sent her to New Orleans, her beloved city. She came back renewed and it would last for a while then she would take another trip to New Orleans and another until they became very frequent. One day, she left in the middle of the night and never came back. She was just gone. Never to return to this place she hated and the family she never loved."

Rose fought back the tears. How could Lisa have chosen something, or someone, in the city to replace this family? A sigh escaped her throat.

Sam grunted. "Sorry about that. I don't usually talk about my problems. Let's get back to the house. I need to figure out when I leave for Mississippi."

"Mississippi? Why are you going to Mississippi? When?" Rose couldn't believe her luck.

"Tomorrow, I guess. Preston and Lewis can't go and I don't trust the twins to check out a combine, yet."

"Sam, do you know how far Sweetwater, Mississippi is from where you are going?"

"Sweetwater? Yes, it's about sixty or so miles, why?"

"I need to meet someone. It won't take much longer than an hour or maybe two at the most. Do you mind if I tag along? If it's a problem I'll drive myself, just point me in the right direction, and I won't be gone long."

"I don't know, Rose. I aim to leave early and didn't plan on any side trips. I need to be back by dark to tuck the girls into bed." Sam removed his cap and scratched his head. He wiped his hands on his jeans and continued his excuses. "I can't be making a lot of stops. This is a working trip."

Rose couldn't believe the sweat as it starting to pool around his neck. Was he afraid of being confined in a car with her? He sure sent her mixed signals.

"It's okay. If you would rather go alone, I'll drive myself. I'm more than capable. Please forget I asked." Rose accelerated her steps.

Sam's footsteps and the sound of him muttering rushed up behind her. Who cared? It was a friendly request, and if he didn't want her company, she would see this mission through alone.

"Wait, Rose. Don't get your back up. I didn't say you couldn't go. I just need to think it through." He fell into step once again beside her.

Silence you could walk on accompanied them back to the house.

"Well I have work to do. I'll see you at dinner." Rose bounded up the steps. Sam caught her by the wrist before she entered the door, ran his thumb over the inside of her wrist and then dropped her hand when he realized what he was doing.

"I plan to leave at six a.m. Be ready."

Sam turned in the opposite direction. His hands shoved in his back pockets, he kicked over a crawfish house as he headed for the rice fields. Never looking back.

I'll be ready, Sam. Will you?

CHAPTER SEVEN

As Rose climbed into Sam's truck, she couldn't help but notice how the inside was neat and orderly. Nothing was out of place. Not at all like her car with empty water bottles and sticky notes in assorted colors stuck all over the dashboard. An mp3 player usually sat on the seat next to her among a lot of candy wrappers, and an overflowing trash bag. This sure told volumes—Sam's life all neat and orderly, hers messy and unorganized. Just one more thing she needed to work on in her life.

Sam jumped in next to her and handed her a basket and thermos. "Odelia fixed us some breakfast and hot coffee. Cups and napkins are in the bag. Do you need a pit stop before we begin?"

"No, I'm fine. Ready to go."

He smelled so good. She realized it was always the same, no matter what time of the day or night. Not like the other men in her life that had taken a bath in after-shave. Sam's natural smell was clean, fresh, like the sheets that Odelia hung on the line to dry. Today he'd replaced the knit shirt that he always wore with a long sleeve button down denim shirt tucked into his nice fitting jeans and no cap.

The blue of the shirt pulled the blue specks from his eyes, leaving the green and brown for added background. But it was the sparkle in his eyes that made her uncomfortable.

The sound of his voice made her jump. How long had she been staring at him?

"Do I have something on my face, Rose? You are making me a little uncomfortable."

Finding her voice took a little work. Blood tingled in her face, burning her neck. "I'm sorry. I was daydreaming. Would you like your breakfast now or later?"

"No, let's wait. I wanted to stop by the bayou, we have a picnic table sat up and it's been a long time since I've been there. The weather is so great, and we've got an early enough start. We can eat and you can tell me all about this meeting you have scheduled."

Mercy, she had forgotten she had to confess about finding the man she believed to be Wilson. She wanted to be far enough down the road that he wouldn't turn back and drop her off at the house. She would have to keep the conversation on something else for a few miles.

Sam pulled up at a picnic table near the bayou. The sound of the water trickling down some rocks in front of the table made a serene sound. The moss on the trees swayed gently with the breeze. Sam was right. It was a beautiful day.

Rose sat on the bench, and Sam settled on the edge of the table. They ate the fried egg sandwiches as they drank their coffee. The fruit they put up for later. As they got back on the road, she asked, "Tell me about the harvest. It sounds like such busy, hard work, but an exciting time." "Hard work? Yeah, it's hard work, but I love it. To see those fields yield what you've worked for that season. We broadcasted the fields in early March and then tended it, flooding the fields, repairing the levees, fighting the blackbirds...all for this moment."

Rose loved the way Sam's enthusiasm filtered through his voice. This was something he cared about passionately. "What do you mean broadcasted the fields?"

"Crop dusters drop sprouted seeds on our tilled soil. The whole process is my favorite time of the year. We try to get a second crop in. Then September till February we flood the fields once again to level the land. That acts as ponds for the waterfowl that migrate every year along with other animals. This process breaks down the chemicals and returns the water to a near pure state so we can return it to the environment." Sam turned to Rose. "Am I boring you with too much detail?"

"You forget I'm a writer, and part of writing is research, and I'm one of those writers that gets bogged down in detail. I had no idea so much went into rice farming. So what do you do September through February?"
"Tend to the cattle, read up on new products, spend more time with my family. After the harvest dance you will see a more relaxed Sam. Now tell me, Rose, who are you going to see?"

Think, Rose, think. What could she ask him about now, was she through stalling?

"He's just an old friend of the family we lost contact with a long time ago." Rose sat quietly hoping this would appease him for the moment.

"Someone you knew? Or someone Odelia knew?"

"Mercy, did you see the size of that bird? What was that anyway?"

"Rose, are you trying to hide something? Who are you going to visit, and why do I feel I don't want to hear the answer?"

She'd been caught. Rose nervously pulled at a loose curl. "All right. You win. But promise me that you won't turn around. Please, Sam, this is very important to me."

Sam was quiet and watching the road. All of a sudden he pulled over onto a dirt road and put the truck in park.

"Rose, what are you up to?"

"Sam, you didn't promise."

"I can't agree to something I know nothing about, but I will promise to listen and be as helpful as I can."

Rose filled her lungs with air and let it go slowly. There was no easy way to tell it but to blurt it out all at once. "You know those letters I've been reading of Aunt Odelia's? Well, I think I've found Wilson. He lives in Sweetwater. I just know it's him. I feel it."

"Does she know about this fool thing you're doing?" Sam's voice was low and controlled.

"No, of course not. I would never get her hopes up without checking it out myself. I don't ever want to hurt her, she's been hurt enough."

"What do you think this will do to her? What if it is him, and he's married? What if he never really loved her and never wants to see her again? What part of this do you think won't hurt her, Rose?"

"She has the right to know. I've thought about this a lot, and no matter why Wilson felt the need to lose touch, she has the right to know. Odelia needs to know. She needs closure to that relationship. If you had never heard from Lisa wouldn't you still want to know what happened?"

Sam held eye contact with Rose, his eyes searched hers for a reason to support her efforts.

"All right. But if he turns out to be a bum, you can't destroy Odelia's dream of that man that left long ago. Deal?"

"I agree, if Wilson is a good for nothing, I'll drop my search. But I can't promise I won't tell Aunt Odelia something. I will promise I won't hurt her. That's the best I can do."

Sam huffed. He broke his eye contact and in a low voice he muttered. "You are a head strong woman, Rose, I know I'm going to regret this later."

Sam started the truck and pulled back onto the road. The silence between them back once again.

"A blue heron."

"What?"

"You wanted to know the name of that large bird, a blue heron. They mate for life you know. So more than likely his mate is dead or he hasn't found the right one yet."

"It's a shame people are not the same. Children would sure have a better life, a more secure loving life."

Sam turned the wheel and the truck exited the road.

"If I remember right, Mr. Herbert's farm is down this road about five miles."

Rose couldn't help notice Sam's easy way with the old rice farmer. He took the farmers hand between both of his and gave it a tight squeeze. Sam's laughter came easy and real as he swung himself into the seat of the combine and started the motor. Then as agile as a teenager, he jumped down and checked the other parts of the combine. Satisfied with the agreement of delivery date, Sam wrote him a check, they shook hands again and Sam returned to the truck with Mr. Herbert right beside him.

"You and your Mrs. are welcome to have lunch before you go," Mr. Herbert called.

"Thanks, but we have to get back on the road," Sam said.

A deep red color of discomfort spread across Sam's face as he sat beside her in the truck and waved his good bye to Mr. Herbert.

"Sorry about that Rose. I saw no need to try and explain."

"No problem. But I do have a question. Why didn't you haggle him about the price? Every man I've ever been with has always haggled, even if it was in a nice restaurant and the food was perfect."

"What jerks the men must have been in your life." Sam looked over at Rose, a deep frown on his face.

She felt small next to him and the questions lingered in her mind. His demeanor was a mixture of anger and pity. "Are you mad at me, Sam?

"No." The word escaped Sam.

"No what, Sam?"

"I was thinking of something else, something I don't want to get involved with. The answer to your question about the price of the combine, I didn't haggle because the price was fair. Look at the map if you don't mind and see what road I take to Sweetwater."

The winding gravel road Sam chose was full of potholes. They finally pulled up to a small neat house with a giant magnolia tree in front. On the porch sat a lone figure.

Sam parked in front and helped Rose out of the truck. The man on the porch slowly edged himself to the edge of the porch and leaned against a post. He shaded his eyes against the sun as he watched them approach. His rocker still rocked as he drew nearer to the steps. He had a definite limp, and Rose knew she had done the right thing.

"Hello, may I help you two young folks?"

Rose's heart almost jumped out of chest. His voice carried itself over her body making her tremble. She thought she would faint, but Sam put his arm around her waist and steadied her.

"Mr. James? Mr. Wilson James?" Rose asked as she peered into a stranger's familiar eyes. Did she know him?

"Yes, who wants to know?"

Words failed her.

Sam took over the situation and introduced himself and then turned to Rose.

Rose took a deep breath and put out her hand for a shake. "I'm so sorry, Mr. James. My name is Rose Ferguson. I was wondering if I could bother you with a few questions?"

Wilson's face paled. "Rose Ferguson, you say? Please come and sit." He limped back up the steps and pulled another chair close to the rocker he'd been sitting in. Sam sat on the steps.

"Let me get us something to drink? I have lemonade in the kitchen. It'll just take a minute." Without waiting for an answer, he hurried into his house.

"Sam, did it seem to you that he had been waiting for someone to come?" Rose whispered.

"Things do seem a little strange. Shh, here he comes."

"Mr. James, I've come to give you this." Rose took the letter Aunt Odelia had written him last Sunday out of her purse and handed it to him.

"Please call me Wilson," He whispered. His hands shook as he opened the letter and read the words, tears flowed freely down his cheek.

Rose knew, then, they had found Odelia's beloved Wilson. The lump in her throat grew, and her chest ached to see this quiet spoken man in such pain.

"I don't understand. This is from my Odelia. Does she know?"

"No, Wilson, I wasn't completely sure you were the same Wilson James. You would be surprised how many men your age have that same name. I've been searching for a while. Aunt Odelia doesn't even know I've been looking for you. She still holds out hope that you will return to her. As you can see by the date on that letter, she has kept her promise to you and still writes you that letter every Sunday."

"My sweet, sweet Odelia. If only." He shook his head then raised his head. "I can't go back. Things are done that can't be undone." He looked into Rose's eyes. "Don't you see?"

"All I see is that two people still love each other very much and time has been wasted."

"What about her husband?" Wilson asked.

"What husband?" Sam asked.

"The one that Ruby told me about. The one I saw for myself when I went to the plantation she and her husband worked on. I saw Odelia and this man laughing with each other. It tore my heart out, but it also pleased me that Odelia had moved on and was happy."

"The only other man to live with Odelia at the plantation was her distant cousin Charles, and he passed maybe five years now," Sam said.

Rose could hardly get words out of her mouth. "What does my mother have to do with this story?" Rose's heart was racing. If her mother had ruined her aunts' life like she had ruined hers, she didn't know what she would do.

Wilson dropped his head. "I can't believe that I messed everything up. After I was injured and knew I would never be the man that left for the war, I felt sorry for myself. They didn't think I would walk again. It took a very long time before I took my first step. I couldn't go back to my sweet Odelia. She was so full of life and deserved so much. And after I did the unforgivable, I guess I wanted an excuse not to face her. My only joy in life has been the knowledge that she was happy. But now I see she has hurt most of her life just as I have. What a fool I've been."

"Then come back with us, Wilson. Tell her the whole story. It's not too late for you. Please come back with us," Rose begged.

"I can't. And please whatever you do, don't tell her you found me. Some things are better left alone. As far as Ruby, it's not my place to tell her story. You need to talk to her. But you will never know how happy I am to have met you."

Rose and Sam said their goodbyes, as rain began to fall. Rose fell in the stranger's arms and held on for dear life. He hugged her as tight as she hugged him. Before he let her go he whispered in her ear, "You are nothing like your mother, Rose. You are a beautiful woman, just like my Odelia. Please keep in touch." Wilson yelled out as they got into the truck. "Take care of her Sam, real good care of her."

Rose got on her knees and gazed at Wilson through the back window as he clutched the letter she had agreed to leave him. Tears fell down his cheeks as steady as the rain down his face.

"He's just like Aunt Odelia described him. And he still loves her so much. You can see it in his eyes and hear it in his voice. I know deep down my mother had something to do with what happened. She can be so evil, Sam, so very evil. I don't think I've ever been so sad."

Rose thought her heart stopped as Sam reached over and took her hand in his. Touching her offering comfort. Her body tingled even if she knew he was just being kind. She pulled his hand up
to her lips and kissed it ever so softly. She held it there against her chest and closed her eyes.

Sam was taking deep breaths, when he tore his hand away and turned sharply onto a dirt road on their left.

"What happened? Why are we on this road?" Rose asked.

"Didn't you see? A black cat crossed the road right in front of us. We can't travel that road now. This road will take us back on our way."

The truck slipped and slid as Sam struggled to keep it out of the ruts filled with mud and rainwater.

"You and your superstitions, Sam. Look at the bad luck we're having now, and a black cat didn't cross this road."

Sam grit his teeth. He couldn't help his superstitions. He knew logically they were wrong, but they'd been such a big part of his life.

The truck came to a sudden stop with the left tire stuck in a hole.

"Stay in the truck." Sam stepped down into the sticky mud and searched for sticks and logs to place under the wheel. When he turned around, Rose was standing beside him, her arms full of branches and sticks. Mud dripped from her blouse and her hands were covered with the dark oozing mess.

"Look at you. Do you ever take orders?"

"Oh be quiet. Start the truck and see if you can work it out of this rut, and I will shove more branches under the wheel."

"No way am I going to let you do something so dangerous."

"I'm not a helpless little girl. Get your butt in that truck. I want to go home and clean up. I've had a very emotional day."

"You are a very stubborn woman, Rose Ferguson. A very stubborn woman."

Rose caught the smile cross his face as he turned around.

Sam started the truck, and Rose stood to the side shoving branches under the wheel. The tire finally caught solid ground and spun, sending mud specks over Rose's face and body as the truck lunged forward and was free.

Rose slid onto the seat of the truck to the sound of Sam's bouts of laughter. "Rose, you look pitiful."

Sam took a rag out of the glove compartment leaned over and started cleaning her face. Rose knew that look, he was looking at the mole on her face again. His lips covered hers, softly at first, questioning. When she didn't pull back, his need increased, deepening the kiss and pulling her to him. He released her lips when she started crying.

Sam released her and fell back against his side of the truck. "I'm so sorry. I didn't mean to force myself on you like that."

Rose began to breathe in short spurts. "You did nothing wrong."

Sam's hands were gripping the steering wheel, "You're crying, Rose." "I did something."

"Yes, you did something all right. I've never been kissed like that before. No one has ever made me feel so needed. You did everything right."

They sat in silence. The rain had started up again and was pelting the truck. When Sam put the truck in gear and put his foot on the gas, it gave a little jump and slid again. "We have to get to solid road." He coughed and, without looking at Rose, his words came slow. "Let me get us safe and then we will discuss what just happened."

The drive gave both of them a time to think. That kiss meant something, Rose was sure. No one kissed another like that unless it meant something. Could it be that Sam cared for her, just a little? She couldn't get her hopes up, she'd been down that road so many times, and was always disappointed. And the concern in his voice made her think maybe disappointment was what he really felt.

Once again on a paved road, Sam cleared his throat. "Rose, I'm sorry. I had no right to kiss you like that. Men have used you all your life, and I refuse to be one them. I got caught up in the moment. You deserve someone that feels deeply for you. And I don't know what my feelings are at the moment. Maybe all I'm feeling is loneliness and lust, and that would never be enough for you. Let's put that kiss behind us."

Rose sat next to Sam listening to the rain and the wipers as they swished water from the windshield. They seemed to whisper "fool, fool." Why was she surprised? What made her think that Sam would be different? Well, it didn't matter. What was the big problem? It's not like she had fallen in love with him? Had she?

Rose bent her chin down where he couldn't see the hurt and   the sense of betrayal, and maybe to give her self-esteem time to return. They would be home soon, and she'd be able to avoid him. She needed time to be alone. To reflect on what today really meant, and to forget that kiss, Sam had.

She forced her mind to something else, but the next thought caused her as much pain. What did her mother have to do with keeping Wilson and Aunt Odelia apart? Did she do it out of spite, or just meanness? Rose intended to find out.

CHAPTER EIGHT

"What in the world happened to you two? Did you have an accident?" Aunt Odelia fussed over Rose and Sam like a mother hen.

"The truck got stuck in the mud, and Rose helped me get it out. That's all." Sam's hooded eyes held Rose's in their gaze. "No one got hurt, right, Rose?"

Rose tilted her head and tore her eyes away. "Everyone is fine, Aunt Odelia. Nothing a good hot bath won't cure."

"Did y'all eat? I made the best gumbo. It won't take a minute to heat. I will not take no for an answer."

Rose turned to walk up the stairs, and Sam caught her arm.

"You haven't said two words to me all the way home. I said I was sorry. If you feel like you have to leave, I'll understand."

"Do you want me to leave?"

"Of course not. But I won't make you stay either. I still need you. For the girls, that is."

"Then I'll stay, Sam. For the girls, that is."

In her room Rose touched her lips. Why, Sam? Why don't you care for me? Rose dried her hair threw on sweats and a cozy shirt and decided to eat in a hurry and maybe she would be through before Sam came back down.

"Sam decided to eat his gumbo before he cleaned up. He's upstairs reading to the girls. Said to tell all good night. He looked beat."

Rose listened to Odelia talk as she forced herself to eat the bowl of gumbo. All she wanted was to turn in for the night and start fresh in the morning.

Sam sat in the rocker on the galley outside his room. Idiot. He knew how vulnerable Rose was, and yet he couldn't keep himself in check from taking her into his arms today. Nothing had ever felt so right and tasted so sweet. But after Lisa, he had to be sure. Was he able to know a woman's needs? Would she love him and Lizzy and Bea enough to stay? He had to be sure. A door creaked. If he stood now and went inside, it would look like he was running away. Best to face the music, they did have to coexist for a while longer.

"Can't sleep, Rose?"

Sam saw Rose jumped and put her hand to her chest. He remembered how soft her hands were when she so tenderly touched his face.

"Warm night." Not waiting for her to reply to his question. "Sit for awhile."

Rose sat on a rocker outside her door, keeping two rockers between them. He couldn't blame her.

"Did you get all that mud out of your hair? We sure were a mess, all because of that black cat. I guess I didn't cross behind it far enough."

"Why, Sam?"

He didn't want to talk about that kiss. He was trying to keep the conversation light. A chill went up his spine at the same time as heat crept into his face.

"Why the superstitions? I've never known someone our age so superstitious."

Sam released the breath he was holding.

"I've thought about that a lot over the years and the best I can come up with is something that happened when I was a little boy. My mother would make up stories around a superstition. How I loved those stories."

Sam stopped rocking and sat on the edge of his chair. "One night we were sitting on the gallery downstairs when we heard a noise. 'That, my dear boy, is a screech owl.' With a sad look on her face, she added 'Someone will die tonight.' She didn't tell me a story that night, instead she took me on her lap, long legs and all." Sam started to rock again, trying to gain control of his feelings.

"She held me a long time singing softly to me. She'd just had the twins about three months when she started to get sick. After I went to bed that night, I heard that dreaded screech owl again. I remember covering my head with my pillow, but I could still hear the owl's cries. Mom died that night in her sleep. Since then superstitions have always bothered me. I know they're not real. But just in case something goes wrong, I follow the rules."

Sam shook his head and realized that he had been talking to Rose about something he never talked about. She probably thought that he was some kind of nutcase.

"I didn't know, Sam. I'm sorry."

"Oh no, you don't. No pity. I'm going to turn in. See you tomorrow, Rose."

Sam waited to hear Rose shut the door to her room but it never came. What was he thinking, sharing all his garbage with her? He knew by keeping the words flowing he would be discouraged from taking her in his arms again. He had tasted her lips and he could never go back to the way it was. Thank goodness he would be extremely busy the following days. But what would he do about the nights

After a restless night filled with nightmares of letters and lonely old men, owls, death and a little boy, Rose was spent. Maybe all of yesterday was just that a nightmare. She could almost make herself believe that if she still couldn't feel Sam's lips on hers. Well, she would not give it another thought. Sam had made it perfectly clear it meant nothing to him, and neither did she.

"Are you coming down for breakfast? Papa ate early and is already in the fields. Bea is in her room reading." Lizzy paused to take a breath. "So are you ready to eat?"

"Yes, I am. Want some company, do you?" Lizzy's warm little hand slipped into Rose's, and together they walked down the stairs. Lizzy lifted Rose's sprit. She could do this, pretend she belonged. After all, she was a pro at pretending.

"Odelia went to check on Susan, looks like we are on our own. I'm already late for my daily news so if you don't mind, Lizzy will eat cereal." Preston grabbed his cap and headed for the door.

"We have Flower Crisp that we can only eat on special occasions, can we have some today, please?" Lizzy begged.

Rose gazed at the small girl all dark curls and sparkling eyes. "Let's see, today is Monday and I am ahead of schedule on my book and I've never had Flower Crisp. Sounds like a special occasion to me." Rose couldn't hold back the laughter at Lizzy's enthusiasm.

"Don't be scared when your milk turns pink, it's ok." Lizzy jammed a spoonful of cereal shaped like little bright colored flowers into her mouth.

Bea joined them at the table, her look full of disapproval. "We're not supposed to eat those, Dad said."

"Your dad put me in charge and he said you could eat them on special occasions, and I've proclaimed this day a special event. So grab a bowl and chow down."

"What's wrong with you today? You seem different." Bea asked as she took a small bite in her mouth.

"I guess I am different. I decided when I got up this morning I was going to enjoy this day. And nobody would cause a cloud to rain on my sunshine day."

"What's a sunshine day, Rose? Can I have one too?" Lizzy's chin dripped the milk she drank from her bowl.

"When I was a girl a little older than you, and I'd had a horrible day, I would play this game with myself and create a sunshine day. All that day I would be happy, no matter what. And yes, Lizzy, you can have a sunshine day, too. Everyone can. It sure helps you make it through this world when you have your share of cloudy days. Now what do the two of you have planned today?"

"I'm not planning to do anything today," Bea responded in her usually grumpy way.

Rose put her hand up and announced, "Okay, if you are going to share my sunshine day, I have rules. The first one is that you can't be grumpy. And the only other rule is you can't think about yucky stuff. So lose the attitude, Bea, and have fun with us. Lizzy do you have any plans?"

"I know, I know, a picnic. Lets have a picnic."

"I've never been on one. That sounds fun. What do we do to get ready?"

"You've never been on a picnic? Where have you been on another planet?" Bea asked.

"No, I've never had the time, but I do now." Maybe Bea was on to something, she sure had an out-of-this-world mother. Rose remembered she had questions for her, but not today. Talking to her mother would surely bring a halt to any sunshine.

"What's all the noise? I could hear the three of you all talking at once. What's going on?" Aunt Odelia entered the large kitchen, fetched her apron hanging behind the door and turned her ever-loving smile toward them.

Why couldn't Aunt Odelia have been her mother? How different her life would have been.

"We're going on a picnic. Come with us Odelia, please? Rose has never been. And this is her sunshine day," Lizzy begged.

Rose and Odelia exchanged a knowing look. "I guess I could go for a while. But I can't stay long. Where are we going?"

"I know a place," Bea spoke up, almost sounding excited. "How about by the old saw mill. It's always cool there, and dad built a table last fall."

"The old saw mill it is. You girls go put on your tennis shoes and get something you would like to do while Rose and I get the lunch ready."

Rose and Odelia spread out the tablecloth and sat the food out. Something was on her Aunt's mind and Rose was dreading the questions. She was trying to put her hurt and disappointment to rest for the day but the memory of that kiss kept returning no matter how much she pretended. The kiss itself might fade for awhile but what Sam had said after the kiss would last a life time.

"Can you tell me what happened yesterday, Rose? You looked so sad when you returned."

Rose's bottom lip trembled. She tucked her head from view.

"I'll tell you sometime, Aunt Odelia. There's not much to tell and right now is not the time. Okay?"

The time together was perfect. Rose and Aunt Odelia played card games with the girls, ate cold roast sandwiches, and laughed until their sides hurt. Yes, this day had been perfect. It couldn't have been better. Even if Sam kept creeping into her thoughts and heart.

Aunt Odelia and the girls decided to make a batch of cookies and Rose headed upstairs to her room.

Following their meeting with Wilson, Rose had decisions to make. Should she tell her aunt about Wilson? Would it do more harm than good? Could it cause Aunt Odelia more unhappiness? Remembering Wilson's kind eyes so full of hurt, pleading with her to keep his secret, was it her place? Rose needed to talk to someone. Someone besides Sam.

Of course, Susan.

The walk to Susan's house helped quiet her fears. By the time she arrived, she thought she knew just what she must do. "Are you sure he's the same man? Can you guarantee that he is Odelia's Wilson?" Susan's face was flushed with excitement. "This is so exciting, Rose. You found him you really found him." Susan put her hand to her mouth. "If I can keep my mouth closed long enough, maybe you can fill me in on all the details."

Rose laughed, as she sat across from Susan and took her hand in hers. She had become so attached to this kind, soft-spoken woman in such a short time. She and Trudy were like sisters to her.

"Oh, Susan, you should see him. He's just like she described him. Tall, handsome and such wonderful eyes, a shadow of that handsome picture that Aunt Odelia still has." Rose could feel the lump blocking her throat. "He didn't know. He didn't know that she was still waiting for him He was heartsick to think he had put her through so much hurt. Her Wilson still loves her,. He's never stopped."

"What did Odelia say?" Susan asked.

"I haven't told her. He asked me to wait. And I decided to give him a chance to make it right in his own time. I can't believe that I have that right to tell Aunt Odelia what I know without the knowledge of the whole story. She needs to know all the details. You know?" Rose stood and poured them each a cup of herb tea.

"Yesterday was such a strange day. So full of hope, but also so full of questions."

Susan searched Rose's eyes. "I'm so glad you came, Rose. You have so much to give this family. Did anything else happen yesterday? Between you and Sam? Don't worry I can keep to secrets to myself.

Rose's voice trembled. Could she trust Susan? Could she trust anyone with her feelings? Rose looked at Susan's face searching for answers.

"He kissed me. Me, Susan."

"I knew it. I knew he had feelings for you. You can see it all over his face when he looks at you."

"Stop," Rose interrupted. "You're wrong. After the kiss he told me it was a big mistake. So you see, whatever feelings you see on his face are not for me."

Rose brushed her hair from her face. "Please don't say anything about this to anyone. I really have to run. I promised Aunt Odelia I would help her, and I am running late."

"Thank you for coming, and do me a favor. Don't sell Sam's motives short. He has some demons to work through. He just might surprise you."

Rose kissed Susan on the cheek. "I'll see you tomorrow." She patted Susan's swelled belly, "I can't wait to see this little one. What do you have, three weeks left?"

"Can't come quick enough for me. Why don't you bring your new book tomorrow and read to me? Remember don't be so hard on Sam. He would be very upset if he thought he caused you any distress."

Rose's brisk steps kept time with her mind. Thoughts flew through her head, if she could just let things go, but that was not in her make up.

CHAPTER NINE

"Rose, is this another sunshine day?" Lizzy skipped along side of Rose as they headed for Susan's house.

"If you want it to be, it can. Lizzy you can choose every day to be a sunshine day if you want. Bea how can you read and walk at the same time?"

Was that a giggle that actually came out of Bea? Maybe she was edging into the girl's world. She decided right then that she would always make an effort to be a part of their life even if Sam didn't want her as part of his.

After getting the girls settled at a table on the front porch with books and paper to draw or write, she turned her attention to the woman that had become so important to her. "You look tired Susan, do you feel all right?"

"I feel great. The baby moved so much last night, I didn't get much sleep. Thank you again for agreeing to sit with me today. I will be so happy when I don't need a babysitter."

"What would you like for lunch? I'll get started." A crash stopped Rose's conversation. Susan dropped her teacup, and a look of pain darkened her face.

"Susan, what's wrong? Are you all right? Please be all right."

Panting, Susan regained her poise. "Good Lord, I think I'm in labor, and my water just broke." Panic, covered her face. "Please send the girls after Lewis."

Rose could almost feel the pain as it raked Susan's body again. Her face contorted with the discomfort. "Labor, you can't be in labor. Not yet, you have three more weeks."

"Hurry, Rose, send the girls. The pains are very close together. Is Odelia at home, or any of the men?" Fear now washed over Susan's face. "Do you know where Lewis is working today? Oh God, here comes another one. Hurry, Rose, please hurry, I need him."

Think, Rose. "Hold my hand, and don't worry, everything is going to be fine."

Rose kept her eyes on Susan's face pinched in pain, her lips turning white as she pressed them together. For what seemed like forever they held onto each other then as fast as the pain came it faded.

"Aunt Odelia went to town for more supplies. I heard Sam say that he and Preston would be in the west field today. Lewis is all the way across the property with the twins working the cattle. Sam's closer I'll send for him. Bea, Lizzy, come here, hurry."

The girls came running and stumbled into the room. Susan's pain apparent as she clutched the pillow she was hugging. Beads of sweat covered her forehead as she gasped for a breath.

"What's wrong, Aunt Susan?" Bea's voice quivered with fear, and her hands trembled.

"The baby is coming. I want the two of you to run and get you dad. Tell him to hurry and send for Uncle Lewis. I've already called the doctor and the ambulance is on the way. Hurry girls, and please be careful." Rose hugged both of them, and watched as they ran down the road. Bea held onto Lizzy's hand and had to keep slowing down so she didn't fall.

Please hurry Sam. I need you. Rose held onto the doorframe.

"Help me." Susan's frail voice tore through Rose.

"I'm here. What do you want me to do?"

"I don't think this little one can wait until the doctor gets here. You are the only one that can help me. Tell me you can do this, Rose. Tell me you won't let anything happen to me or the baby."

Rose stared into her friends pleading eyes. *I can do this. I have to do this.*

"Don't worry, I did a lot of research on childbirth for one of my books. You and the baby are in good hands." Now if she could just convince herself. "Stay calm. I'm going to get some towels and alcohol I'll be right back."

Please let me do this right. Rose prayed.

Rose held onto the cell phone as she dialed the doctor's number again. An answering machine picked up. The doctor was away on an emergency. *I pray that we're that emergency.*

Susan clenched the sheet that Rose covered her with and let out a moan as pain after pain raked across her. "Deep breaths, Susan, and just think this is the day a new Leblanc is about to enter this world. Think you can handle that?"

Susan laid her head back and closed her eyes. "I knew it would hurt but not this bad."

"I know, sweetie, just hang in there. It'll be over soon.

"Oh, God, here comes another one," she yelled.

"We can do this, Susan." Rose said as she checked her progress. "There's the head. I see the head. A small head covered with dark curls, just like the mama's."

Susan was getting weak. Her eyes were closed and her hands were shaking.

Rose had to rush things alone. "Push, sweetie, push. I've got the baby."

"What are you doing? Wait for the doctor." Sam's voice was a higher pitch than usual, and he was out of breath.

Rose turned slightly to see him walking to the bed. "You stop right there, Sam Leblanc. Don't come any closer. You're covered in dirt and germs." She turned back to the job at hand. "Just stand over there and keep quiet. One more time, okay, Hon? One more push."

The baby slid out into her hands. "It's a girl, Susan. A beautiful tiny little girl." She laid the small wrinkled baby on Susan's body and started to clean the mucus out of its nose and mouth. A small cry grew louder followed by the sound of four men as they ran into the room. The wail of a siren could be heard in the distance.

Lewis headed for his wife but was stopped by Sam. "Rose said we couldn't get close as dirty as we are. Neither Susan nor the baby needs an infection." Rose could hear the happiness in Sam's voice as he talked to his oldest brother. "Congratulations, big brother, you're a dad now, and I'm here to tell you there is nothing like it."

She lifted her head and looked at the five large men standing with their hats in their hands not bothering to wipe the tears that streaked their dirty face. Rose had never known men so in touch with their manhood that they were not afraid to show their emotions, tears and all.

"Lewis, run jump in the shower, and you can ride with your family in the ambulance," Rose said as she stood and washed her hands in the pan of water. A lone curl fell free and eased across her face, she had never been so weary.

After the doctor cut the cord and examined Susan, Lewis came running in, hair still wet, shoes untied, and a grin as big as the sky on his face. He went to Susan and wiped the damp strands of hair off her forehead.

"Everyone is fine," Susan said as she touched Lewis's hand. "Thanks to this little lady. Had she not been here, I think we wouldn't be celebrating right now."

All eyes once again on Rose, her face reddened. "Thanks, but all the glory goes to Susan, she did all the work."

All four uncles, Rose, Bea, Lizzy and Aunt Odelia stood on the porch and watched as the ambulance took the happy little family away.

"Come on girls, ride with us to the house, and we can all get ready to drive to the hospital. Come on, what are we waiting around for? We have a new family member to greet." Preston motioned for everyone to pile into the pickup.

"If it's okay, I would like to walk." Rose said softly.

Sam walked the girls to the truck and said something to Preston then walked back to Rose as they drove off. "I've decided to walk with you. He stuffed his hands in his pockets as he walked beside her. "You are a woman full of surprises, Rose. I would never have thought you could deliver a baby. Thank you for jumping in and taking charge. That was a very brave thing to do."

Rose felt her lips began to quiver and she stopped by the water's edge. Her body began to shake and the increasing lump in her chest threatened to close her throat. "I didn't feel brave. I was so scared. So terribly scared. What if something had gone wrong? What if..."

"Come here, *bebé*."

Sam gathered her into his arms. His wonderful safe arms. Rose allowed herself to be held. If only time would stop, and she could stay in them forever.

She buried her face in his shirt and inhaled his scent. How could someone's scent bring such a physical reaction? Her head lay on his chest close to his heart, she could not only hear it but she also felt the beat. Was it beating for her? This is where she belonged if only he felt the same. What she would give to be a part of that little baby's life. But he had never even thought of that. Rose pulled away and steadied herself.

"I'm fine now. Let's go see that baby and find out what they named her."

Sam's saddened eyes turned away from Rose. "It's okay to take some time for yourself. You were under a lot of pressure." They walked the rest of the way in silence.

"You know I am very proud of you, Rose. My family will never forget what you did today," Sam said as he left her at her bedroom door.

Are you Sam? Are you proud of me? Something to make you see me as more than just a mess up? I hope so.

Rose stood outside the window of the hospital nursery, amazed as the newest LeBlanc family member stretched her tiny arms and wrinkled her little nose. "She's perfect," she whispered.

"Yes she is. Thanks to you. Susan and I will never be able to repay you for your actions today." Lewis put his big arm around Rose's waist. "Have you heard her name?"

"No." Rose could hardly breathe. Nothing had ever happened to her like this. So many people approving of her at one time was almost overwhelming.

"*T-Sou.* Which translates to little Penny. She's our good luck, don't you agree? Her full name is Penny Rose LeBlanc."

"Thank you, Lewis. I don't think anything ever made me this proud. Do you think it would be all right if I go in and see the little momma for a moment, I know she lost a lot of blood and she must be tired."

"She would have my hide if I didn't make sure she got to visit with you tonight. You know, Rose, even before today she told me on a number of occasions what a good friend you have become to her. Let's go see if my beautiful little momma is awake."

Rose stood inside the door as Lewis eased to his wife's bed and bent down and ever so gently kissed her.

"Hey little momma, you got company." Lewis never took his eyes off of Susan.

Love seemed to fill the room. Susan lifted her arm weighted down with an I.V. and brushed his dark curls off his forehead and peeked through the crook in his arm.

"Hey, Florence Nightingale. You still running around, you should be in bed after what you did today. Did you see Penny? Isn't she the most beautiful baby in the world?" Susan held her hand out to Rose.

Rose noticed that Lewis had slipped out and they were left alone. "She's just perfect, Susan. Thanks for naming her after me, I will have to be a very strong role model."

"I don't think you'll have any problem with that job. I can't wait to get home with her. I've been in that bed so long, but she's worth every bit of the long wait. The doctor said that I would be strong enough to go home in a couple of days." Susan stifled a yawn.

"I promised myself I would not stay too long, so I'm going to go now, but I'll be back tomorrow. You get some rest, because from what I saw of Miss

Penny, she is going to be a handful."

Rose stood, but Susan stopped her from leaving. "Rose, I don't know what to say about today..."

"Words aren't necessary. We'll talk about it for years to come I'm sure. You get some rest."

Rose walked out of the room and leaned against the closed door. *This is what I want, the marriage, the husband, the baby, but most of all the love that I've witnessed today.*

CHAPTER TEN

The week flew by running between Susan's house and trying to keep up with Bea and Lizzy. Finally the day arrives to begin the harvest.

"Come along, Rose. This is a sight to see. One that never ceases to excite me." Aunt Odelia tugged on Rose's hand, her face lit in a childlike enthusiasm.

They stood on the gallery, arms linked, and watched as the combines positioned in a straight line waited for the signal. They stood four across manned by Lewis, Preston, Randy and Sam.

Rose thought she moaned out loud when Sam climbed up in the seat of the cab. A grin spread across his face so large she thought his lips would split. You could tell by the look on his face this was the moment all the hard work led to. Rose half-expected him to yell out "wagons ho" and lead those monster machines into the valley.

Sam leaned out his window and with his arm extended waved the other three to follow. The giant machines marched along, securing the rice from its plant. Dust rose in their path, and the smell of earth and plants filled the air.

"Isn't that a wonderful sight, Rose? Little grains of rice pay for all of this and provide a living for everyone here. Can you imagine? A little grain of rice."

Rose and Odelia worked side-by-side all morning preparing the food they had cooked earlier. They had to transport the food to the outdoor covered eating hall close to the fields. The long building had a tin roof with several ceiling fans cooling the room. Large screen windows spread out across the walls allowing the outdoors in.

Bea and Lizzy helped set the long table that was flanked with benches on either side. Ten places were set and waiting for the men and their appetites. A large side table held a pot of steaming gumbo dotted with bits of chicken, sausage, and okra. Another large pot held white fluffy rice, bowls of crackers, and a huge container of potato salad kept cool by cracked ice completed the bulk of the noon meal. Four pies cut in healthy slices filled the end of the table. Pitchers of ice tea dripped their moisture on the long eating table along with jars of pickles and peppers. A bottle of Tabasco hot sauce sat by every place setting.

The rumble of the machines quickened Rose's heart. Laughter grew louder as the workers approached. The outdoor sinks with running water were soon buzzing with activity. Washed and hungry the men sat around the table. Plates passed, food served and the talking became a low murmur.

"Hey, little Rose, what pie did you bake? I bet it's the sweetest," Randy teased.

"Odelia, who did you think you were cooking for, a bunch of Yankees? I've used almost half this bottle of Tabasco, and a baby could still drink it from its bottle." Preston held his spoonful in the air. He turned to the tall blond man next to him. "Speaking of Yankees, how are you holding up Mansir?"

"Don't worry about me, Preston, MaeMae burned the first layer of my tongue off months ago."

"Thank goodness you didn't like the gumbo, Preston, you only ate four bowls." Odelia teased .

Rose brought Sam a piece of pie and was met with a wink. "Thank you bebé," he whispered.

Mixed signals. Sam was a master at mixed signals. But for today she would glow in his attention.

The evening meal was much like the noon meal. Hurry in, hurry out. With the combines put away, the tired and happy workers left for their own homes promising to return the next day, while Sam and his brothers returned to the big house.

Rose didn't see Sam after he read to the girls. He disappeared into his room for an early night.

"Well what do you think?" Aunt Odelia patted Rose on her arm.

"Rice harvest is more exciting than I thought it could be. Everyone working together, pulling for the same result, life couldn't be much better than that. I think I'll turn in Aunt Odelia, if you don't have anything else for me to do, I'm beat."

"Get a good night sleep, Rose, we have the same schedule tomorrow. Rest well."

After a long hot bath, Rose towel dried her hair and sat on her bed trying to focus on revisions but with little success.

A soft knock on the French doors broke her concentration. Sam leaned against the frame when she opened the door.

"I saw your light. Want to sit on the gallery? I'm too keyed up to sleep."

His hair was damp and tousled from a recent shower, he wore jeans with no shirt, and his feet were bare. He never looked better. A slow grin picked at his lips, but quickly disappeared with a frown.

"If you're too tired, I understand." He turned to walk away.

"Wait, Sam, let me throw on a robe. I'm not sleepy, either."

The night was unusually cool for the summer, and a faint fragrance of fresh earth drifted on the breeze. The moon darted in and out of the clouds, giving a mystic feel to the night. They sat in rockers and silently enjoyed each other's company.

"We had a good day. This crop is going to yield more than I thought. I think it will surpass last year's. Each year is different. You worry that you'll get too much rain, or too little. You worry if the price for rice will be enough to make up your cost. I can't tell you how great it feels to see all the hard work you did pay off. You know?"

"Yes, I do. I feel the same after I complete a book from start to finish and see it on the shelves in a bookstore. Each book holds a piece of me in it, and it makes me proud when a reader tells me that it made a difference in her life. Some of them I've worked on for a year or more."

Sam stilled the rocker, rested his hands on his legs. "I had no idea Rose. I guess I never thought about the work that went into writing a book. You really hear from people that buy your book?"

"Yes. I'm just starting to build up a readership. That's why this book is so important, to keep up the momentum. Not all are good comments, but most are. And sometimes I get that rare one that touches my heart."

"Huh," Sam grunted.

Sitting beside Sam and listening to him talk about his day was a dream come true to Rose. *This is what I hoped a relationship would be.* Sharing. And even without saying a word, enjoying his company.

"If the rest of the harvest goes like this one, we'll finish in record time. Then it will be time to plan the harvest dance. It will be over before you know it Rose."

They returned to their silence. Rose tucked her feet under her robe and folded her arms across her chest. Yes, it would soon be over. What would she do then? Find a place to live nearby? Or relocate to a new place? The thought of leaving her new friends and family made her sad. A chill washed over her.

"Are you cold?"

"What? No, not really. Just thinking. It's about time I make plans for where I'll go after you don't need me for the girls. My book is almost finished, and I need to find a place to settle." Rose stood from her chair and started to her door. "I think I'll turn in, another big day tomorrow."

"Rose, wait." Sam put his hand on her arm. "You could stay."

"No, I'm tired. I'll see you tomorrow."

"I mean after the harvest. You don't have to rush off somewhere," he said, his voice husky. "Stay."

His fingers gently rubbed her arm. He raised his eyes to hers. Searching. As if in slow motion, he drew her into his arms and lowered his lips to hers. This time, he took her lips slowly, softly nibbling at her bottom lip then moving to cover both. His mouth seemed to have a mind of its own caressing, nibbling, and sucking hers, while his arms held her close. So close she couldn't tell which heart beat was hers.

Rose tried to breath, to move, to think. But was afraid to do anything. "I'm yours Sam." She wanted to yell, but she was lost to his wonderful lips.

As fast as it started it stopped. Sam held her at arm's length. Their breaths came in short spurts. "What am I doing? You make me crazy. You know that? I think we both better turn in before we both do something we would be sorry for in the morning. Night, Rose."

Rose felt her swollen lips and blinked back tears as she stumbled into her room.

I make you crazy, Sam. What do you think you do to me? She wanted to scream. *I don't have to put up with this. I won't put up with this.*

Rose marched out her door and found Sam leaning against the railing of the gallery. Storming up to him, she poked her finger in his chest.

"Don't toy with me Sam. You make up your mind about your feelings and let me know if they positive or negative. I will not, you hear me, not be put through another emotional relationship and be left out in the cold."

Sam opened his mouth to speak, but was silenced with Rose's glare.

"Not a word. Not tonight. Remember what I said. Either you want me as I am or you don't. There is nothing in between."

Rose hurried into her room on shaky legs, locked her door, crawled under the quilt and turned out the light.

Men. A sense of satisfaction settled on Rose. Let him stew on that a while.

Sam knew he had to sleep or tomorrow would be a killer, but try as he might he couldn't shake Rose's words. What were his feelings for her? It had been two years, no, longer, since he had a woman to love. Lisa had turned away from him awhile before she left, claiming one ailment after another, and he had been too hurt to trust another woman. And his girls consumed a lot of his time after Lisa left. Did he even have the time to pursue a relationship?

Sam got out of bed and took the few steps to the bathroom down the hall. He hesitated at Rose's door. *Are you asleep, Rose? I have to sort things out about you heaven knows you deserve better, but now is not the time.* He would wait until after the harvest, *his mind would* be clearer then, and maybe he would know what the heck was going on with his body.

His desire was never to *hurt* her. He knew she'd been through enough, but that was exactly what was happening. *I'll have to control myself that's all.*

The word desire flashed across his mind once again, along with the sweet smell of her still on him, and the feel of those soft, giving lips, still lingered on his.

Sam let out a low growl and covered his head with his pillow. "You drive me crazy Rose, completely, utterly crazy," he said into his pillow.

The scowl on Sam's face at breakfast told the tale of his sleepless night.

"What the heck happened to you, brother? You look like you snuck out and tied one on. You could at least ask us to go along," Preston teased.

Sam raised his head and glared at Preston. "Mind your own business. Don't mess with me today, I'm ..." Sam stopped in mid-sentence when Rose spun on her heals and disappeared out of the dining room. She wore a deep frown on her face, not her usual smile.

Did he look as sad or frustrated as she did? It appeared neither had gotten much sleep.

Rose came back to the table and retrieved her coffee cup, she was in desperate need of another cup of coffee.

She glanced over in time to see Preston give Randy a wink and a nod of his head in her direction. Tears burned the back of her eyes and she took her coffee outside and sat on the porch swing.

The early morning dew glistened on the grass, and a calf bellowed in the distance, probably searching for its mom. The moss on the trees swayed to an unheard waltz, and the birds welcomed the morning with a song. This was life at its best without the bustle of everyone hurrying around with tasks to do. Just the sounds of the morning welcoming a new day filled with new promises.

The weight of someone as that sat on the swing next to her brought her back into focus.

Preston put his large hand on her shoulder. "I'm sorry, little Rose. I sure didn't mean to give you the impression I was making fun of you. I'm real sorry."

"Preston, it's okay. You didn't do anything wrong. I'm just tired. Didn't get enough sleep last night, that's all. After a few more cups of this strong coffee I'll be good as new." She tried to display a reassuring smile but her lips wouldn't cooperate.

"Well, you know and I know that's not all that's going on. If you need a strong shoulder to cry on, or someone to talk to, or hell if you need someone beat up, I'll be happy to take care of that too."

Preston reached over and gave Rose his customary bear hug. The kind any little girl could curl up in and feel protected. And the best part she knew he meant every word he said. It was good to have him on her side.

"Thank you Preston, but this is something I need to work through myself. I have a lot of thinking to do, and quite a bit of planning. But thank you so much for caring. You and your family mean so much to me."

"Don't forget what I said, you're family. And heck we are all attached to you. Even Sam. Especially Sam. He's slow to catch on sometimes. Give him time."

CHAPTER ELEVEN

At the end of the first week of harvest, Rose was both proud and sad that she had succeeded in keeping her distance from Sam. He was as cross as a bear anyway. His brothers tried to tease him into a better mood to no avail. Lizzy and Bea were the only two that brought a smile to his lips.

Rose missed their late night talks on the gallery and the playful flirting during the meals. Most of all, she missed him. His smell, their stolen kisses, the feel of his arms around her were all still too real to her.

Alone in her room, she waited for sleep to come and when it didn't she crept to the French doors and opened them just a crack. She peeked around the doorframe and saw the gallery was empty. Sam must be asleep. It was only when she heard voices coming from his room that she realized his door was open, she made haste to return to her room when the voices grew angry.

"Sam, I want to go to the police academy. I just don't love rice farming the way you do. I feel I'm needed elsewhere."

"I told you, Preston, I'm not keeping you here. You are free to go anytime, but you are chasing a dream. This is where you belong. Think man. Think about what all you have here. This is your dream, if you would just open your eyes, don't you see?"

"This is not my dream, it's yours. Just forget it. I'm going the day after the harvest dance, so get used to it. It's not me leaving that has you so bent out of shape. We all know what's bothering you, and if you're not careful you are going to mess up big time."

"Suit yourself. But you're the one making the mistake, one huge mistake."

Rose listened to the door close. She turned from her eavesdropping place and headed for her bedroom.

"Get an ear full, Rose?"

She swung around to face Sam, her heart pounding. The moon slid behind a cloud, and Sam's face was shielded from view. She couldn't see the anger in his eyes, but she could hear it in his voice.

"Sorry, Sam. I only overheard a little and was trying to escape to my room. Goodnight."

"Oh, no you don't. You wanted to know what my conversation was about, by all means sit and I'll fill you in. It's so much easier than sneaking around."

Sam's breath warmed her cheek as he stood closer. He smelled of fresh pine soap. She could almost feel his arms around her. If wishing were so, he would reach out and draw her to him. Could he hear her heart? *What's wrong with me, he's done it again.* Made her forget what she was truly feeling. She was mad, and he needed to know it.

"I don't sneak, and I resent you implying such. Your voices were loud, so of course I heard some of your conversation. Enough to tell you I agree with Preston. Why do you insist on keeping everyone here? Under your thumb? Maybe Preston has his own dreams and they are not the same as yours. Maybe this place doesn't hold the same attraction for him as it does for you. You can't keep people here against their will, Sam." She stepped inside her room. "Goodnight, Sam," and closed the door and clicked the lock. How arrogant. She crawled into bed and tried to still her shaking shoulders by pulling the covers tighter around her.

I could just shake you Sam. No one frustrates me more. She turned over in bed and punched her pillow. "I just need a good night sleep," she muttered. "That's all I need."

Except you, Sam, I need you.

The noon meal went off without a problem. Rose was impressed how organized Aunt Odelia handled each and every thing. The food was always the right temperature, the menu simple but tasty. She had come to love the flavors in the Cajun food. What a good Cajun cook could do with a roux was unbelievable.

"How do you know you've made a good roux Aunt Odelia? You never seem to measure anything."

"Honey child, you can't over plan a roux. You have to feel it, smooth under the weight of your hand. It takes a lot of attention and a willing heart. A good roux has to have good body and just the right amount of spice. Not too hot but hot enough."

Laughter poured from Aunt Odelia. "Mercy, it sounds like I'm talking about a man don't it?"

"Okay what did I miss? I went inside to make a phone call and returned to both of you giggling like school girls," Trudy said.

"Aunt Odelia made a comparison of a good roux to a good man. Very clever." Rose winked at her aunt. "You should be the writer in the family, not me."

Trudy pulled her hair back into the ponytail like the one she had worn earlier giving her a softer look, almost child like. "I guess we don't have much time to rest, what are we doing for supper?"

"Don't worry about the time. Preston cooked barbecue chicken and ribs, and the salad, red beans and rice are already cooked. So let's visit."

Aunt Odelia stood to go inside. "I'll make us a fresh pot of coffee and we can talk away the rest of the afternoon. I have something I want to tell you anyway."

When the three women settled on the gallery, Odelia pulled a small crescent bloom out of her apron pocket. "Look what *Tante* Ina left me." She held the bloom up and said, "Preston told me she likes to leave someone she likes a message, that they did something she liked or that something wonderful was about to happen to that person. So I'm waiting to maybe win the Lottery."

"Really," Rose said. "So now I know why she left me two of those blooms after Penny was born." She laughed. "So since I'm still short and not famous she must have approved of me helping Susan birth Penny."

"Well I feel left out. *Tante* Ina's never left me anything, maybe you have to be family."

Then Trudy recanted a story of one of her clients in the funeral home causing another bout of laughter. Rose knew she would miss this friendship on a daily basis when she had to leave.

The three women's laughter stopped as quickly as it started when they all saw a lone figure of a man walking down the road leading to the plantation.

"He must be someone lost or selling something." But then Rose could see his limp and the way he carried his lean tall body. She opened her mouth to speak again, but the shattering of Aunt Odelia's cup as it hit the porch silenced her.

"It's him," whispered Aunt Odelia. She put her hand over her heart and stood on visible shaking legs. "Oh, dear Lord, it's him."

"What is it Odelia? Do you know that man?" Trudy asked.

"It's Wilson. Don't you see? He's come back to me, it's my Wilson."

She took a deep breath and clutched her hands to still them from shaking then started the decent down the stairs.

The man walked a little faster, until his gate was almost a run. Rose wiped the flow of tears trailing down her face. "Please don't let him hurt Aunt Odelia with his secrets, she whispered."

The couple reached each other and fell into each other's arms. Both sobbed quietly. For what seemed like hours they clung to each other then pulled apart both keeping their hands together. It was like watching an old movie when two lovers were about to be separated and held on to each other for dear life. Each afraid to let go.

"You are still that beautiful woman I said goodbye to so long ago, you haven't changed a bit." Wilson said.

"Then you've lost some of your eyesight," Odelia laughed through her tears.

"I wasn't just looking at you with my eyes, Odelia. I was looking at you with my heart, and there you will never change. You will always be my sweet, beautiful Odelia."

She released one of Wilson's hands and reached up and caressed his face. No one existed in the world for the two old lovers except each other.

Wilson held on to Odelia leading her gently toward the porch where the two could sit.

Rose motioned to Trudy, and they slipped inside the screen door, neither ready to take their eyes off the miracle of true love. After all these years, the love between them could be seen all over their faces.

The women lingered at the door for a moment, then Rose shut the big wooden door leaving the two old friends to catch up on a lifetime.

"Fess up, Rose, you had a part in this didn't you?" Trudy perched on the arm of the overstuffed sofa in the living room, her eyes bright with questions.

"I located him on the Internet, and when Sam went to Mississippi to buy that combine, I talked him in to taking me by Wilson's house. Of course, I didn't know at that time he was Aunt Odelia's, Wilson. I didn't think he would come, he said he wouldn't, that the past needed to stay in the past. But I guess his loneliness caught up with him. He wouldn't tell us why he never returned to Odelia, but it has something to do with his injury and my mother." Rose tucked the stray curl behind her ear. "Can you believe it? If I find out my mother deliberately did something to keep these two apart I'll never speak to her again."

Rose curled up on the other end of the sofa facing Trudy. "Surely he's mistaken, don't you think?"

"I don't know, people can do crazy things to each other. But he's at fault, too, he never even answered her letters."

"He didn't know, Trudy. I brought him a couple of Aunt Odelia's letters and he wept. They never got to him. He was in a hospital, and I guess someone in his unit sent all his mail back with an address unknown mark on them. It's all such a mystery. I don't know how she kept her hope alive all these years."

Trudy slid onto the couch and kicked off her shoes. "I think somewhere there is that kind of love for everyone, don't you?"

"Lord, I hope so. After Ted dumped me, I thought no love existed like that. I gave up all hope of ever finding someone, and maybe I won't. But now I know, for some people, strong pure love is there, and I'm not ready to give up hope that it exists for me."

###

Sam sat with his brothers and field hands enjoying the barbeque. He tried in vain to concentrate on what the rest were talking about, but his attention was drawn to Rose. Her jeans fit in all the right places, and her tee shirt pulled across her chest as she bent and straightened her body pouring tea and refilling empty plates. He hadn't talked much to her since that night on the galley. Of course, she was right, he had no right to toy with her. He dropped his arms in his lap; they ached to hold her against him.

Sam shook his head. What was he thinking? He didn't go and fall in love with this woman, did he?

Rose bent over and placed a plate of bread in front of Sam.

"Where's Odelia? Is she sick?" Sam knew his words had come out sharp, but she annoyed him. With her soft skin, large green eyes, and that slight smell of fresh peaches that lingered in the air long after Rose left the room. Ahh. She made him crazy.

Sam looked around the table forcing his eyes away from her, settling in on Trudy.

"Well, Trudy, you sure look pretty today. Can you tell me where Odelia is? Rose seems to be out of sorts."

"She has a visitor, and we told her we would take over this meal. Thanks for the compliment even if it was second-hand." Trudy put her hands on her hips, daring Sam to make any more comments.

Sam raised his head in time to see Preston give her a wink and a nod of his head in Sam's direction.

"Preston if you are through maybe you could help Randy put his combine up. Do you good to leave the table and food behind."

"I don't need anyone's help, I'm not a child." Randy stomped out and climbed into his combine muttering all the way.

The hands headed to their homes and Lewis fixed a plate for Susan and said his goodbyes.

Sam stole a look at Rose and started in her direction when Preston stopped him.

"We need to talk, little brother. We need to talk now."

Machinery put away, Sam and Preston walked toward the house.

"Say what's on your mind, Preston. I want to visit with my girls."

Preston stopped and faced Sam. "All right. As your family, we think you either have to come to grips about your feelings for Rose, or go away somewhere so we can get the harvest in."

"You're crazy. And what do you mean we? Y'all have been talking about me behind my back?" Sam pulled his cap off and beat it against his leg. The heat in his face felt like a deep sunburn.

"We think..."

"Never mind what all of you think. I don't have feelings for Rose. She just makes me uncomfortable. Always prancing around with her red hair and wide eyes. So stop this nonsense and let's go wash this dirt off."

"Sam, wait. Why are you so bent on not admitting to yourself how much you like this woman? Everyone knows. Everyone can see. And besides that, you are making all of us miserable. What's holding you back? She fits right in. The girls like her okay. And look what she did for Susan and Lewis. Hell, we are all very fond of her."

Preston smiled his slow smile, "If you don't want her, let Randy know, he's kind of sweet on her."

"Rose is not like an old baseball mitt that I would hand down to my younger brother. Randy gets a crush on anyone with a soft touch. Tell him, never mind. I'll tell him that Rose is way out of his league. Now that this crazy talk is over, let's go clean up." Sam shoved his cap back on his head and headed to the house.

"Rose did look good today, didn't she?" Preston asked.

Sam heard the question, but knew this one didn't need an answer, Preston was thinking out loud as he often did. Could Preston be looking at Rose in a different way these days? He'd had almost the same heartbreak as Sam, except he had only been engaged to his first love when she broke his heart. Since then, he'd never gave another girl a second look, except maybe the girl in Bon Amie that he refused to talk about.

Sam knew that this big old teddy bear of a brother would make the best husband and dad of all of them. It would take that special woman. Sam stole a glance at Preston, trying to read his expression. Everyone deserved to be happy, didn't they? At least once.

"I guess I had my chance."

"What? Are you talking to me?"

"No, I think we have talked enough tonight."

"All right Sam, I'll let it go for now, but think about what I said and make sure whatever you decide you don't hurt Rose in the process."

Sam huffed and hurried inside.

Odelia met him at the bottom of the stairs. The man he and Rose had met in Mississippi at her side.

"Sam, I think you have met my Wilson, but I needed to know if he could stay for a while? I put him in the spare bedroom by the sun porch." She gazed up at Wilson. "We have much to talk about after all these years."

Sam held out his hand. "Good to see you again. I'm glad you took Rose's advice. You are welcome in our home as long as you want to stay. Feel free to make yourself at home." Sam hugged Odelia and headed up the stairs. "Night all. I think I have two little girls upstairs needing a hug." Heaven help him he knew he needed a hug too.

The thought of Odelia and Wilson arm and arm still with him. After all this time love still danced in their eyes. Sam shook his head and opened the door to Bea's bedroom.

"Hey princess, did you have a good day?"

Bea put her book down and pointed to the lump in her bed. "Hey, Dad. Yeah, but I think Lizzy isn't feeling too good."

Uncovering the lump, he found Lizzy all curled up asleep, her cheeks flushed with fever. "Still crawling into bed with you I see."

"I don't mind. She's not ready to sleep in her own room yet. Don't make her, okay?"

Sam loved her ever bit as much as he loved Lizzy. When Lisa left, he thought Bea would never smile again. But there she sat smiling that sweet smile and caressing Lizzy's hair, like the small caregiver she was. He admired Bea. Rejected twice, once by her birth father and second time by her own mother. Never again. If he had to move heaven and earth. Never again.

"All right, princess. But maybe we need to see about a bigger bed for you." Kissing Bea on the forehead he headed for the bathroom. "I'll be right back, let me get something to knock that fever down."

Lizzy opened her mouth and took the meds without a whimper turned over, hugged her doll and never opened her eyes.

"What are you reading? It seems lately you always have a book in your hands." Sam knelt beside Bea's bed.

"A book Rose bought me. I'm so glad she came Dad, she's taught me a lot about books. I even think my reading is getting better. Rose says the more I read the better I'll get." Bea sat on her knees. "Rose says that I can be a writer too, if I want too. She said I could be anything I wanted to be. She also said someday she would like to take me on a trip to New York and take me to a show. A real life Broadway show." Bea hugged Sam's neck. "Do you like her dad? Lizzy likes her a lot. Do you?"

Sam swallowed hard. "I think she's a real nice lady. Lay down now and don't forget to breath. I think you said all that in one breath. If Lizzy feels bad tonight come and get me, okay?"

"Okay, Dad. Love you."

"Loved you first."

CHAPTER TWELVE

Odelia was at the stove humming some song, and stirring something that smelled wonderful. She reached around for the pepper off the table as she spoke to Rose.

"Lizzy is running a fever and her stomach hurts, do you mind saying at the house with her? Bea is old enough to help set up dinner for the guys, and Trudy is here."

"Not at all, Aunt Odelia. I have some catching up to do on email to fans, and I still have the last two chapters of my book that is due, past due."

Her aunt had a spring to her walk and a glowing smile across her face. "Did you and Wilson get all caught up on the past?"

"Ah, Rose, it's like he never left. And if I have my say so, he won't leave again. Not without me." She straightened the bun on her head and sighed.

"Are you blushing? Did he tell you the whole story? Can you share it with me?"

"Honey child, he did tell me the story, and someday soon we will share it with you. He has some things to sort out first. Don't you worry yourself, everything will be fine." She bent and gave Rose a kiss on her cheek, then grabbed the plate she'd fixed and put it on a tray with a magnolia bud tucked in the napkin. "Now if you will excuse me, I think Wilson needs breakfast in bed this morning. He's come a long way."

What are you hiding, Aunt Odelia? Something was behind that smile and it looked like sadness. Rose made herself some toast and a cup of that wonderful dark roast coffee, and headed upstairs.

Lizzy was curled up in her bed. Bea was already helping Trudy.

"Hey Lizzy. Why don't you and Miss Abby come curl up in my bed and we can talk and tell stories, it's very soft and big. Will you let me carry you?"

Lizzy put her little arms around Rose's neck and laid her head on her chest. She looked so small in Rose's big bed. Rose fed her some of the toast and sips of water then watched as Lizzy snuggled down with Miss Abby and fell asleep.

"You have come to mean a lot to me, little one," Rose whispered and kissed the soft cheek of the sleeping child.

For one so small you have wormed your way into my heart, as did the rest of this family. Rose put her thoughts to her work at hand.

The morning flew by, and Rose felt good about the work she was able to accomplish. She was more pleased that her mind was engaged in her hero's and heroine future, which kept her from fretting about hers.

"Miss Rose, I feel better."

Rose crawled into the bed with Lizzy. "Push over. May I hold Miss Abby?"

The well-loved doll showed soil on her face and yarn hair. "When did you get Miss Abby?"

"Daddy gave her to me one Christmas. He said his mother made her for one of her children, but all she had was boys. So he said she saved it for me." Lizzy gave the doll a big hug and handed her to Rose.

"You can hug her if you want. Miss Abby don't mind. She likes to love you back. Did you ever get a doll like Miss Abby for Christmas when you were a little girl?"

"No, my mother gave me a doll every now and then, but not the kind you could play with. They were all dressed up in very fancy clothes and had porcelain faces." Rose pulled the yarn hair out of Miss Abby's face as she remembered.

"My mother always reminded me not to mess them up. 'They are to look at and to appreciate their beauty' she would say."

"Did you get your dolls in a box wrapped in red paper and a big gold bow, under your Christmas tree?" Lizzy's voice echoed the excitement of a child remembering a fun time.

Rose handed Miss Abby back to Lizzy.

"Sometimes they would come in a box with a bow, but I never had a Christmas tree. Mother said they were a waste of time and just made a mess. We had a tree at one of the schools one year when I couldn't go home for Christmas. My mother was out of the country, so I stayed at the school. That year she sent me a hat that was too big. She said we would go shopping when she returned, but we never did."

"Yeah, my mommy gave me one of those dolls one time. She was real pretty, but she was cold and hard, not soft and warm like Miss Abby." Lizzy climbed into Rose's lap. "Mommy didn't like Miss Abby. Just like she didn't like me or Bea." Lizzy contemplated Rose. "Do you like me, Miss Rose?"

"Aw honey, I like you a whole bunch. I think you are a very special little girl. And don't tell grumpy Bea, but I like her too." Rose hugged Lizzy to her and smashed Miss Abby between them. *Neither of us deserved not being loved enough by our moms, Lizzy. Neither of us.*

Rose thought she head someone at the door but when she looked up no one was there, but she knew she heard footsteps as they walked down the stairs.

"Well, did you check on Lizzy?" Sam asked Preston.

Preston stood before Sam, hands stuffed in his back pockets as if to hold them at bay. "Lizzy is fine. Why wouldn't she be, she's with Rose? I'll tell you this once, little brother, and only once. If you ever hurt that woman, you will have me to reckon with. You understand?"

"What the hell is wrong with you? Hurt what little woman? You have been out in the sun too long." Sam yanked his gloves off and tucked them in his cap. "Let's eat some lunch."

"You heard me, Sam. Don't you dare hurt Rose, she's been hurt enough." Preston turned and climbed back onto his combine, cranked the motor and headed back into the rice field without lunch, leaving Sam to puzzle over their brief conversation.

Sam looked toward the house, should he check on Rose? He shook his head. If something were wrong, Odelia or Trudy would let him know. Being in the same room with Rose would tie his insides in a knot, and one good day of work would finish up the harvest. Then he would be free to explore the feelings he had about Rose.

Trudy met Sam at the lunch table. "Where's Preston? He's usually the first to arrive and the last to leave."

"He's got a burr under his seat about something. I'll bring him a sandwich when I go back to the field." Sam fixed his plate and sat at the end of the table.

"Trudy, did you happen to see Rose this morning? Was she all right?"

"Odelia saw her and told me she was chipper as always and seemed kind of excited about spending the day with Lizzy. Why?"

"No reason. Something Preston said." He stuffed a bite of mashed potatoes in his mouth and tried to settle the spot in his stomach that was tied in a knot.

Bea came over with a full glass of sweet tea. She wore one of Odelia's aprons that had to be folded over several times to fit her tiny frame.

"Who's the new help, Odelia? She sure is a pretty little thing," Sam teased.

"Ah, Dad. Don't make me spill this tea in your lap."

"I'd tip you extra to see that, Bea," Rusty said.

"You would have twice as much to do today if that happened, Rusty." Sam took another bite. "Think we can finish up today boys?"

"We might have to work a little later, but I think we should give it a try. I would love to spend a full day with my baby and wife." Lewis smiled through the grime on his face.

Trudy appeared with a covered plate full of food and a thermos of tea. "Don't worry about bringing Preston a sandwich. I fixed him a plate."

"Time's a wasting, let's go." Sam loved every bit of this life. The hard work just yielded success. And this time of the year brought them all together.

The harvest dance was a bittersweet ending. They would have brought in a good crop, this year better than last year, and would have a few months off to re-group. But it also meant the twins would be heading back to college, and who knew where Preston would go. The harder he tried to hold on to things the way they were, the more things changed. Maybe it was for the best. Maybe Rose was right. Everyone deserved his own dream.

"Come on, Sam. You going to daydream all day?"

"I'm not daydreaming, just thinking. Let's get this crop in."

"How do you feel Lizzy? You sure look better." Aunt Odelia sat on the rose chintz chair in Rose's room and watched as Rose and Lizzy put a puzzle together. "Bea's home and I know she would love to tell you about her busy day, and from the looks of things, it appears that you and Rose had a busy day yourself."

"I feel good. Rose made me all better. Is it okay if I go and see Bea, Miss Rose?" Lizzy pushed one of Rose's curls out of her face.

"You bet. We can work this puzzle another day. Maybe Bea would like to help us." Rose pulled Lizzy in to a hug. "See you later. Oh, and you almost forgot Miss Abby."

"I didn't forget her, I think she needs to stay with you until bed time." Lizzy skipped out the room like she hadn't felt bad all day.

"Well you must have scored some points today with Lizzy. She never lets Miss Abby stay over with anyone. I'm glad to see you are getting along so well with the girls. They needed someone like you to fill their cup with joy." Aunt Odelia leaned back in the chair. "I think I'm going to go to my room and rest for a while. Dinner's easy tonight. Cold fried chicken, potato salad, green salad, and some other leftovers, that way they can eat when they are ready. This might be a long day."

Aunt Odelia stood and moved to the door, hands on her hips. "Rose, I just left Wilson on the gallery down stairs. He said something about a walk. Why don't you join him, you've been cooped up all day."

"I think I will, it looks so beautiful outside. Will you need me for anything?"

"No, child, I think Wilson needs you more than I do at this moment." Odelia kissed Rose on the cheek and walked down the hall humming her made up tune.

Why would Wilson need her? Rose tied her shoes and bounded down the stairs. She found Wilson on one of the porch swings with his legs stretched out and his eyes closed.

The sound of her footsteps caused him to open his eyes and he met her gaze with a timid smile.

"Hey, sunshine. What are you up to?"

"Aunt Odelia said you might want company for a walk."

Wilson shook his head. "That woman. She always knows what other people need before they do. Mind walking with a slow old man?"

"Not at all, the slower the better. That way we can see more." They walked down the lane leading away from the plantation. The same lane Wilson had walked down a week ago.

"Are you sorry I found you, Wilson?"

"Sorry? Heavens no. I found my sweet Odelia again because of you. The only regret I have is that it took me so long to face my fears. The time I have wasted being prideful. If you see happiness within your reach, grab it, Rose. Don't think about if it's the right time or if you deserve it, grab it." Wilson bent and pick up a long stick and used it as a walking stick. They walked in silence.

"Wilson, tell me about yourself."

"What do you want to know?"

"Do you still work at a job? Aunt Odelia said you had some business calls the other day."

"I'm a freelance writer, and I still write a weekly newspaper column for the same newspaper I've written for the last twenty years. I also take assignments for magazine articles. I always wanted to write that breakout novel but never could get it off the ground."

Rose had stopped walking and was watching Wilson talk about his writing. She knew exactly how he felt.

"I'm a writer, too. I write fiction, and I love it. Wow, I would never have guessed. Although that one letter Aunt Odelia let me read that you wrote to her was so beautiful, I should have guessed. Tell me more, what kind of novel?"

She and Wilson sat on a log beside the road and talked writing for almost an hour. Never had she met someone with the same ideas and love of writing as Wilson.

"Now tell me about you, Rose. Are you happy? Did you grow up happy?

What a strange thing to ask. But somehow she knew he really wanted to know. Maybe Odelia put him up to finding out about her happiness.

"I'm happy. I found out a long time ago no one person can make me happy, but me. Was I happy growing up? Not always. But somehow the time passed and I coped."

"Was your mother kind to you?"

"My mother? That's right you knew her. She never hit me or anything. She tolerated me, is the best way to describe my mother's attention. The less time she had to spend with me the better on her part. But she always sent me to the best schools and dressed me in the best clothes." Rose drew in a breath and held it for a moment then released it slowly.

"I haven't thought of this in years, but Billy Joe, a boy I once loved, told me that Mom did all of those things for me to make her look good. At the time, I thought he was just jealous he couldn't give me those things, but the more I thought about what he said, I knew he was right. All the clothes and schools were for her, not for me at all. She's not a very loving person, Wilson."

Wilson put his arm around her shoulder and whispered, "I know."

Her hands began to shake, "you said that my mother had something to do with you and Odelia breaking up, is that true? Please tell me the rest of your story?"

"Soon, I promise I will soon, Rose. Now let's go see if those men have finished their harvest."

Did she really want to know the whole story? Something deep inside her told her no. Silly thoughts, what could her mom possibly have done so horrible to break up Wilson and Odelia?

"Tell me something? Have you always loved my aunt? Even when you returned her letters?"

"I never stopped loving her. Remember that. She was and still is the love of my life."

Wilson slowed the pace as if to hold on to their time alone.

"Now, tell me more about you. What's your favorite color, do you like music and if yes, what kind?"

"Hmm, my favorite color is yellow. Reminds me of sunshine and the beginning of a new day. As for as music, I like all kind, but classical music is my passion. It soothes me somehow, and I love to write with music in the background. Of course, I'm partial to Chopin." Rose looked over at Wilson, who had the strangest look on his face. "What? Do you hate Chopin?"

Wilson cleared his throat. "No. In fact, he is one of my favorites." He touched her on the arm and started the long walk to the house.

The sun was beginning to sink behind the mighty oak trees, and Rose could hear the hum of the combines as they completed their job. She stole a glance at Wilson and was met with those familiar eyes staring back.

"Thanks for the walk, Rose, but most of all thanks for the talk. We'll talk again soon." They stopped on the gallery and Rose headed for the swing. "Are you coming in?" Wilson turned around waiting.

"No, I've been in most of the day. I think I'll sit here for a while. I'm trying to form the last two chapters in my book. They still are not working for me."

Wilson grinned. "It'll come. I have no doubts. I read your other books. They're good. But I think this one will be the best."

Rose couldn't keep her eyes off of the man as he limped inside. He'd read her books. Why would he take an interest in her books? The screen door closed behind him. She wished she could be as sure as Wilson sounded as he talked about her work. No doubt about it, this book was pushing all her emotional buttons, and she wasn't quite sure why.

Wilson found Odelia in the kitchen. She faced the other direction and didn't see him come into the room. She hummed a song, one he remembered from a happier time. Lord, how he loved this woman. And he vowed he would not mess up this second chance.

He walked up behind her and put his arms around her ample waist. "Hey, beautiful." He felt her relax in his arms.

"Hey, yourself. Did you have a good walk?" She turned in his arms and met the kiss with one of her own.

"I can't believe I get to hold you in my arms again. My sweet, Odelia. You are so beautiful."

She smiled. Then giggled. "It's a good thing that memories have bad eye sight. Love is most definitely blind. Tell me about your walk with Rose, did you find out anything?"

Wilson walked over to the table and sat in a chair, pulled another close by and patted the seat for her to take next to him.

"If I wasn't convinced before, I am now. I need to tell Rose what I suspect, and soon," he said.

Odelia took his hand and held it in hers looked him in the eyes and smiled. "Will you look at that, hands both wrinkled and worn from time, but still strong. Just like our relationship."

He brought her hand up to his lips and kissed it.

"Do you mind if we talk to her together? But can we wait until after the harvest dance? I need to put all my energy into that right now."

"Of course not. But we need to tell her. That girl needs a lot of love to make up for all the love she lost out on. A lot of love."

CHAPTER THIRTEEN

The sound of a combine came closer. *Someone finished early.* Rose had mixed feelings about the harvest coming to an end. She was happy that Aunt Odelia and everyone else didn't have to work such long hours, but it also meant she would be leaving soon. It was time she made a decision. She needed to find a place to call home and start new. But where?

"No place could feel like home without a family. My family," Rose muttered.

"Talking to yourself?" asked Rusty.

Rose jerked her head up and saw Rusty standing on the bottom step he held his cap in hand, with tousled hair, giving him a boy like persona, but his build gave his age away. This was no boy, but a man with still some growing up to do. But heck didn't everyone have some growing up to do?

"Hey, Rusty. Didn't hear you come up. You worked in warp speed today?"

Rusty took the steps two at a time in an easy stride. He pulled up a chair across from Rose and sat. "Mind if I ask you a few questions? I could use some advice."

"You want to ask me questions? Well, sure. But don't you think Aunt Odelia, Sam, or any of your other brothers could give you advice?"

"Heck no. You are just the person to give this advice."

Rusty dug the toe of his boot against the leg of the chair making a grinding noise. "You see, there's this girl."

His face turned a tinge of red. He lowered his eyes, and then took a breath, gathered his nerve and looked Rose in the eye.

"I've liked Shelia ever since I was in grade school, but I always knew she was out of my league. She's a model for Pete's sake. Her family moved away when we were juniors in high school, but this past year they moved back. I just found out she is here for the summer. Something about an illness."

Rusty leaned forward, his elbows resting on his knees. "Here's the thing, Rose. I want to invite her to the harvest dance but I don't know what to say. I never had this problem at college. Is something wrong with me?"

Rose sat back and chose her words carefully. Flattered that he was asking advice from her. "I think you don't have a problem asking other girls out because they don't mean as much to you as Shelia does. What do you mean she's out of your league? Have you ever asked her out? Or let her know how you feel?"

"I don't know. I guess I think someone that beautiful would laugh at me if I asked her to go somewhere with me. And no, of course, I never asked her out."

"You listen to me, Rusty LeBlanc, you are a very handsome man, and very sweet. You have a lot to offer a woman. How do you know she hasn't felt the same about you all these years and you've missed out on being with her?" Rose took both of Rusty's hands in hers.

"Ask her Rusty, she won't laugh at you, I promise. Maybe she'll say no, but maybe she'll say yes. You'll never know unless you ask"

A slow grin crossed Rusty's face, a grin that resembled Sam's, just not as wide.

"You're the best, Rose. I think I'll go clean up and go ask her in person. You think?"

"I think." Rose said. Smiling Rose added. "Oh Rusty, take it easy on the after shave, and ask Aunt Odelia if you can pick some of the gardenias. After all, you heard she was not feeling well. Good time for a visit."

Rusty almost ran into the door as he tore inside.

Rose felt like a big sister helping her younger brother. It felt good. No, it felt great.

Rose tucked her feet under her and leaned back in the swing. A quick smile pulled her lips.

"A girl would have to be crazy to not say yes to you, Rusty," she whispered.

Her thoughts turned to her book. Was Rusty the kind of hero her hero was turning out to be? No, not enough confidence. More like Sam. Comfortable in his own skin, Sam. Afraid of commitment, Sam. Warm and gentle, Sam.

"Penny for your thoughts."

Rose jumped as his words scattered her thoughts.

There he stood, right in front of her, wearing that sideways grin. Dust covered his close fitting jeans that clung to his muscular legs giving them definition. But his face drew her attention the most. Dirt mixed with sweat had found a home in the cracks of his laugh wrinkles around his eyes and in the frown wrinkles on his forehead.

The two faces of Sam. The happy family man and the dubious man afraid of trust. Could he read her thoughts, did he know they were about him? Those searching eyes of his could probably see right into her heart. Did he know how often her thoughts turned to him? How often her heart ached for him?

"Problems, Rose?" Sam sat in the chair that just moments before his brother had vacated.

"No, why?"

"You looked so far away. Did Lizzy give you any trouble today?"

"Lizzy? Gracious no, she is such a sweet little girl. You have done a remarkable job with those two girls. Bea can be kind of grumpy sometimes, but she seems to be happier lately. She so enjoys reading. I see a lot of myself in Bea."

Heat spread from her neck to her hairline and she knew she was blushing. What on earth made her say that?

"Not that she should be like me, I certainly didn't have anything to do with her birth, nor her childhood. I didn't mean to sound like..." Rose witnessed as Sam's grin broke into full-blown laughter that rang out into the evening.

She couldn't help but embrace his light mood.

"Please stop me Sam, I'm talking and I can't stop." Rose's laughter mingled with his.

Sam put his hand on her knee and both stopped laughing and looked into each other's face. She could feel the heat from his hand and she knew it wasn't hot because of the temperature.

"Rose, I have a question to ask you." Sam's voice deep and husky held the tension that she felt.

"What?" Her voice squeaked as she spoke.

"Yeah, well, I wondered if you would go with me to take the girls shopping for something new to wear to the harvest dance? I know girls like to get all dolled up for parties. Maybe you would like to buy something new too.

"Sure, sounds like fun. When?"

"Tomorrow? If Lizzy is up to it. The dance will be at the end of this week."

"Sounds like fun. I'll be ready." Rose stood and stretched her cramped legs and arms. Was that a groan she heard from Sam? Surely not, but the look on his face confirmed her thoughts.

"I hope I don't disappoint you, Sam."

Sam lifted from the chair and stood facing her, so close she could smell his scent.

'Why do you think you'll disappoint me, Rose? Are you fixing to be bad?" Sam placed his hand in his right pocket and jiggled his keys.

A sign, Rose had come to recognize that Sam was out of his comfort zone.

"Helping the girls pick out something to wear, of course. I don't have a reputation as a great fashion expert, in fact just the opposite according to my mother."

"I disagree. You always look very put together to me. Not too dressed up and not too..." Sam stopped in search of his next words. His grin spread further and red colored his cheeks.

"Sam! What are you talking about?"

They stood on the gallery just inches apart both in their own thoughts. He was looking at her lips again, until she couldn't catch her breath. If he didn't grab her soon and let her kiss him, she knew she would have to make the first move. As she bent in to meet him half way, he licked his lips and reached for her. The anticipation was causing her to take her breaths in short gulps. Hurry Sam, hurry. Her mind willed him to kiss her now in front of whoever came around.

Lizzy broke the moment as she rushed to Sam and threw her arm around his leg. "Papa, are you through? I feel better. Rose took good care of me. Can we do something special tomorrow, Papa?" Sam jerked his look from Rose and turned it on Lizzy. Leaving her to collect herself and return her breathing to normal.

"I was just asking Miss Rose if she would accompany us to shop for some new rags for the dance. What do you think?"

"Papa, you silly, we can't wear rags. Are you coming Miss Rose? We will have just the best time if you come, say you will, please."

"I've already told your dad that I would love to go. I think I'll let you two do the planning, and I'm going to take a shower. See you tomorrow."

"Can I go tell Bea? She's going to be happy too."

"Sure, pumpkin. I'll see both of you at dinner. Don't forget to wash you hands."

Lizzy rushed around Rose and tore into the house yelling for Bea.

"Thanks, Sam. Let me know about the time and I'll be there."

"Rose, don't go. I'm sorry if I made you uncomfortable, we still need to have a talk."

"Not now, Sam, I have to go. I have a lot of thinking to do."

He searched her eyes for answers but finally lowered them. " I'll let you go for now, but we will have that talk and soon."

Rose turned her back and he grabbed her arm.

"Rose, one more thing you have to know. I could never be disappointed in you."

"Never say never, Sam."

Rose stood outside her bedroom door, hand on the doorknob the feel of Sam's touch still on her arm. Tears stung her eyes.

"Rose are you all right? You look like you are about to cry."

Rose jumped and turned around. "You startled me, Aunt Odelia. I'm fine, a little tired, that's all."

"Hon, why don't we go in your room and have a nice visit. We've been so busy I've missed talking to you. You go on in and let me grab a cup of coffee for each of us."

Rose sat in the overstuffed chair in the room that had been hers for the length of her stay. Deep depression set in. Why did she feel so sad?

Odelia knocked softly on the door then entered holding a tray.

"Now talk to me, and don't tell me nothing is wrong, I can see it on your pretty face."

"You make me feel like I was caught with my hand in the candy dish." Rose could feel the tears start and knew there was no stopping them.

"Aw, honey, it'll be okay, nothing can be that bad." Odelia drew Rose to her and hugged her tight, allowing her to cry.

Between gulps, Rose tried to talk.

"I didn't try to...I didn't want to..."

"Want to what, Rose. Take your time. Drink your coffee. We've got plenty of time."

They drank coffee in silence. Rose could feel her insides settle down. Feel the confusion start to leave. But the sadness stayed.

"Fall in love with him," she whispered. "I only came here to find a way to start a new life, never did I think I would make a fool of myself again. How can I be so stupid, Aunt Odelia? I know better than to think someone like Sam could love me back."

Rose wiped her eyes and raised her head and looked in the eyes of her kind and beloved aunt.

"I know I have to leave soon, but I don't know if I can. You see, I've grown to love this whole family."

"Why? Why do you have to leave, honey? You know you are welcome here as long as you need to stay. And as far as Sam, don't be so sure he doesn't share your feelings. I see how he looks at you. Give him more time; he'll come around."

Rose shook her head then took a big sip of her coffee. "Do you really think Sam has feelings for me?"

"Time will tell, honey child. Time will tell."

Odelia let out a heavy sigh and offered a weak smile. "Now tell me how's that book coming?"

"Not bad. I'm almost through and I think it might turn out to be one of the best I've ever written. And I owe most of it to you and Wilson. Without those wonderful letters and the love the two of you share, the book would not have turned out."

"You just need to believe, Rose. That's all, believe." Odelia stood, and patted Rose on the back. "And don't give up on love, never give up on love."

"Well it's been a long day and I have a date with a tall handsome man. You sleep well my little Rose, and remember how much you are loved."

###

"Are you awake Miss Rose?" Lizzy whispered from the other side of the closed door.

"Not only awake, but fully dressed and ready to shop." Rose flung open the door. "Have you had your breakfast?"

"Yes. All of us have. Except you, but we can wait until you eat. Papa said we are in no hurry." Lizzy tilted her head to the side. "You look pretty today, Miss Rose. All green and fresh." She giggled. "Your shirt even matches your eyes. I wish I had green eyes. Not these old dirt eyes."

"Why, Lizzy. You have beautiful eyes. Who in the world told you your eyes looked like dirt?"

Lizzy twisted her shirttail between her fingers. "Promise you won't tell Papa?"

"Of course. Not if they hang me by my fingernails." Rose smiled trying to make light of a subject that had turned serious all of a sudden.

"Mamma. Mamma use to tell me all the time she wished I had her eyes, they were blue like Bea's. Mamma said mine didn't have a shine, they were the color of dirt. She said I took after the LeBlanc family."

"Ah honey, I'm so sorry, my mother use to say hurtful things to me too." Rose sat on the floor and took Lizzy onto her lap.

"You know what I think of when I look into your eyes?"

"What?"

"Warm, rich chocolate. And you do have the LeBlanc eyes. Look at the picture of your grandmother that sits on your daddy's desk. You have her eyes, Lizzy. Warm, friendly, and kind eyes. I think you are very lucky to have such beautiful eyes."

Lizzy hugged Rose tight then gave her a wet kiss on her cheek. "I'm going to see that picture. You eat so we can go. She turned and ran back to Rose still sitting on the floor. "I love you, Miss Rose."

Rose watched Lizzy skip down the hallway and heard her bounce down the stairs.

Parents say horrible things to their children. In one sentence they can mark them for life. If given the chance, she would do a better job than her mother, a much better job.

The four of them shopped and laughed, ate and laughed, held hands and laughed. Never had Rose felt more complete. Like a family. Today she would allow herself to pretend. Today she was part of this little family.

Bea and Lizzy came running up to them each holding an ice cream cone. Lizzy stumbled and dropped some of her chocolate ice cream on Rose's white pants. "I'm sorry Miss Rose."

Rose looked into the big tear lined eyes of Lizzy. "It's just ice cream honey, it'll wash out. And if it stains I will always remember this day every time I wear them."

Lizzy smiled and she and Bea asked if they could go and play for a while. Sam agreed.

"Let's sit here and let the girls run and play in the park. Here, you better see if you can get most of that off." Sam handed her his handkerchief and motioned to a bench under a huge mimosa tree.

"Thanks for helping me. The girls are so happy with their clothes. I would never have thought Bea would choose something so bright. She's usually so conservative. Jeans and a t-shirt, that's her style."

"Maybe she's trying to grow up a little. This is a hard time for girls. A little girl in a maturing body. Changes. Get ready for the tears. The next eight years should be interesting. Lizzy's the easy one. Let her dress like a princess. If it is shiny and it sparkles, then she's happy."

Sam sat staring at the woman who in a short time knew his girls better than he did. A tinge of guilt crossed his heart.

"You know them well, Rose. I should have been paying more attention."

"No, Sam. I don't really know them as well as you do. But I do think I have had the same feelings and needs."

Sam watched Rose as she spoke so lovingly about his daughters. It was time to make a decision. A decision of the heart. He had to take Rose in or cut her loose. He had to decide what was best for Bea and Lizzy.

CHAPTER FOURTEEN

The house had been in such a bustle all day. The preparation for the dance had excitement dancing through the air. Every nerve in Rose's body was alive. This had been a strange week. Sam had worked very hard not to be alone with her, but flirted with her continuously. He had made her promise to give him the first and last dance.

Rusty was floating around the house with the knowledge that Sheila would be in his arms tonight and no one else.

Preston walked around the house singing.

Wilson smiled at her under sad loving eyebrows, and Aunt Odelia hugged her a lot. Love and secrets filled the air.

Sam took in the sight of Rose as she descended the stairs. The deep green sundress showed off her eyes and the bounce in her red curly hair gave softness to her face. A smile rested on her lips and a natural blush covered her cheeks. But it was the tilt of her head and the way her eyes held a confidence that took his breath away. "Wow, you look so...great. I mean beautiful. I want to take you in my arms and kiss you breathless."

Smiling, Rose winked. "If you're nice. I might let you have a tiny kiss."

Sam's heart jumped. "You make me feel alive, Rose. So alive," he said, his voice husky. "Let's go show these people how to dance, because if I keep you to myself much longer, no telling what I'll do. You have no idea what effect you have on me."

"Oh, I don't know Sam, if it's anything like the effect you have on me then we might be in trouble." Rose grabbed his arm and they all but ran outside to the large tent.

The tent housed a large dance floor with table and chairs. Food lined the back of the tent on long table. The live band consisted an accordion, a washboard, a singer and a beautiful woman playing a fiddle. Sam told Rose her name was Joelette and she was married to Mansir. The music started, and a few couples hurried onto the dance floor.

Rose glided into Sam's arms for a perfect fit. She was sure her feet never touched the floor.

"Where did you learn to dance like this?"

Sam grinned. "Surprised? Mom taught all the boys but the twins. She believed that dancing was love in motion, and she wanted all of us to be able to do it well. Some of my best memories of my mother were our dance lessons. Every time I dance, I feel she left me with a part of her."

Sam tucked Rose under his chin and swept her away. She could feel the rhythm of his heart as it mixed with hers. His arms held her tight, his feet driving them across the floor to the beat of the music. Every now and then, he planted a kiss on top of her head. This was a perfect night, a perfect time.

One song ended and then another. With the next song, Sam guided them into a more private part of the dance floor. He held her closer and began to sing the slow Cajun words of the song in a rich baritone voice. If she died tomorrow, she would die happy. His voice touched a part of her no man had ever touched. It was a song filled with words she didn't understand, but the tone in his voice told of sadness and longing. Her throat began to close up and a hint of tears threatened. God how she loved this man.

At the end he leaned down and kissed her ever so softly on her lips.

"Meet me after the dance in my room. Please." His voice begged.

"I need to tell you something, Rose. Somehow we will make this thing between us work. You won't be sorry. Meet me, Rose."

"Yes," was the only word she could say? "Yes, yes, yes."

"Yes what, Miss Rose?"

Lizzy and Bea stood next to Rose and Sam, their world suddenly filled with other people.

"Yes I'm having a great time. Are the two of you having fun?" Rose answered.

"We want to dance." Lizzy said.

"Dance with us Papa."

"Why don't we all dance together Lizzy? Me, you, Bea and Miss Rose?"

The music started and once again Rose felt a part of this wonderful little family. Their laughter rang out in unison as their feet went in different directions.

All of a sudden Bea stopped her face froze.

Rose followed Bea's eyes as they glared at a woman standing near.

A woman no one could miss. She stood with the light shining above her head, illuminating her golden hair and stunning face.

"Hey baby, got a hug for me?"

Bea glared at the woman, still holding onto Rose and Sam's hands. Rose could feel her little body shaking.

Sam cleared his throat and took Bea by the shoulders and pointed her toward the beauty.

"It's ok honey, go tell your Mom hello."

Bea pulled back.

"It's okay, I'm right here," he reassured.

Rose's head began to clear. The beauty standing with her arms open was Lisa, the girl's mother. Sam's wife. She let go of Sam's hand and looked up at him. Searching his face. Hoping for instructions. He frowned.

"I'm sorry Rose."

Sorry? Sam was sorry. Had she lost again? Yes, of course she had. But this time it hurt worse. Worse than she'd ever hurt before. Tears filled her eyes as she looked through them at Sam's wife. Bea stood stiffly in her arms, Lizzy held onto Sam's leg beside Lisa. Rose followed up Sam's frame and settled her gaze on his face. A face so full of turmoil, she had to look away. Moments before she had felt the most happiness ever. Now she was empty. Spent. Totally alone. Unable to bear her sadness any more, she turned and fled to the sanctuary of the house. Away from the gaiety of the music and people. Away from the reunited family, Sam's family.

Somehow she reached her room, she leaned against the closed door. Gulping back the sobs that raked through her body. Once a fool always a fool. How could one person always fall for the wrong man? How could one person always be the one to walk away empty handed? How could one person start to believe in happy endings, only to have them torn away and destroyed?

Rose spied her beloved snow globe, and in one swift motion picked it up and sent it flying across the room into the fireplace. The globe shattered into a thousand pieces. Rose bent down and through her tears picked up several shared pieces.

"Just like my life," she whispered. Rose picked up the small plastic couple from the smashed globe in her hand.

"Just like my life," she repeated.

Rose heard the soft knock on her door and the footsteps behind her.

"Ah, honey." Trudy knelt beside her and put her arms around her. "I'm so sorry, Rose. No one thought she would ever come back. No one." Trudy continued to talk to Rose in a very low voice, soothing, cradling her in a light rocking motion.

"Cry, Rose. You cry all you want. Life is not fair and you have had your share of the bad parts. So get it out, doll. Get it all out."

Rose tried to talk but the words froze in her throat. "I don't—" she gulped. "I don't think I'm strong enough to put the pieces back together. Not this time."

"I know that globe was important to you, but maybe we can glue it back together," Trudy whispered.

Rose raised her head and looked at Trudy. "I'm not talking about the globe, Trudy. I don't think I am strong enough to put my life back together. None of the pieces fit anymore. Don't you see? Sam was the one. Sam was the only one that could have given me my happy ever after. So the pieces are shattered, and I can't put them back. Not this time."

Rose allowed Trudy to hold her for a while. So tired. Rose was exhausted. "I think I need to rest, Trudy. Thanks for the shoulder to cry on, but I need a place to shut my mind off. Do you mind?"

"Of course not, Rose. Take all the time you need. I'll spend the night tonight, so if you need me just holler." Trudy got up from the floor and helped Rose and then kissed her on the cheek.

"You are like a sister to me, so remember I love you and will always be here for you. Can I get you something before I leave? A drink, something to eat?"

"No, I don't need anything. Thanks Trudy."

Rose paced around the room in a trance. Her eyes hurt from the hard crying and the pain in her chest made her weak. She turned back the covers and crawled in to bed with her sundress on. Maybe, if she closed her eyes, all of tonight's happenings would turn out to be a nightmare. But she knew as she turned off her lights tomorrow she would have to make plans. Clutching the plastic couple in her hand she sobbed into her pillow.

Sam paced outside Rose's room. How could things have changed so fast? Three hours ago, he held Rose in his arms and thought he would still be holding her. After all this time, Lisa was back. A changed woman, so she said. She said she loved and missed the girls. But he'd also seen the lack of trust that showed in their eyes as they listened to her apologize and make new promises.

He would never forget the hurt in Rose's eyes when she left the dance floor. He'd never meant that to happen. Never did he set out to be the bearer of such pain.

Sam moved in front of her door again and pressed his ear to the frame. Not a sound. Was she okay? He had to find out.

"Rose, are you awake? Rose," he repeated.

He knocked softly.

"Go away, Sam," Rose whispered.

She was at the door. He could feel her presence. "Please, Rose. Let me in. We need to talk, please."

The lock on the door clicked and Sam entered the dark room. He could barely make out her small figure curled up in the chair beside her bed. He sat on the floor in front of her, willing his hands not to reach out for her. He reached up and turned on the lamp sitting on the table near her. As his eyes adjusted to the light, the vision he witness was that of a small girl who had been rejected too many times. Her head was bent her eyes closed. She looked so small. Remembering the happiness on her face earlier this evening when they danced, and seeing it red and swollen from her tears tore his heart out.

"Aw, *bebé*, I never meant to hurt you. Never in my life have I been the cause of such pain to another." He reached for her hand but she drew back. "Please don't think I didn't mean those words tonight. I needed you Rose, I still do. If Lisa had not returned, maybe."

"Maybe? Maybe what, Sam?" Rose met his look. Her eyes were cold, empty, abandoned. "What would you have done, Sam? If Lisa didn't return?"

Sam searched Rose's eyes for a clear answer. The lump in his throat grew with pain.

"I don't know, Rose. How could I know? I never thought she would return. But now she has and I have to do what is right for the girls, I have to think of Bea and Lizzy." He took a deep shaking breath and whispered. "If it was just me, Lord knows I would not even hesitate. But now I just don't know."

Pulling his eyes away from hers, he shook his head. He couldn't stand to see such pain in those beautiful green eyes anymore, he bowed his head.

"I just don't know," he whispered.

Rose placed her hand on his head entwined her fingers in his hair and gently lifted his gaze to hers again.

Sam felt his chin quiver and as the tears slid down his face, his heart breaking.

"Then I guess we have nothing left to say to one another." She continued to run her fingers over his hair and gave him a weak smile. "It's okay, Sam. It's not your fault."

Rose leaned over and kissed him lightly on the lips.

"Now if you would please leave my room, I have plans to make and I have to get some sleep."

Sam continued to peer into her eyes. "Are you leaving us?"

"Please, Sam. If I stay here any longer I'll die. Please? Let me go." Letting out a long sigh she whispered. "You can't have both of us, you know."

Sam left Rose's room with the weight of a heavy chain around his heart.

"How could everything have gotten so messed up? What will I ever do without you, Rose?"

Rose was up and packed before the rest of the house was awake. The night had held no sleep for her, and with the sounds of Sam's pacing coming from his room, he'd been up all night.

A soft knock at her door broke her thoughts of Sam.

"Hi, hon. I thought you might be up and thought the two of us could have breakfast in your room."

Aunt Odelia hurried in carrying a tray of food and coffee. Leave it to Aunt Odelia to know just what Rose needed.

As they ate and chatted neither mentioned last night.

The food had smelled so good when her aunt brought it in, but as Rose put it in her mouth, she couldn't swallow the food as it stuck in her throat and her stomach churned.

"I'm sorry, I thought I could eat but I can't."

"Okay, drink your coffee and listen to me tell you a story. I know you are not in the mood, but this is something you need to hear."

Aunt Odelia took a sip of her coffee and settled back in the chair.

"Wilson wanted to tell you, but I thought after what happened to you last night you needed to hear this from me. You remember Wilson telling you that your Mom had something to do with Wilson not coming back to me? Well this is the whole story. When he got wounded and was in the hospital in Washington, your mother went to see him. She told him I had met another man, married him and was happy. She convinced him I would be better off with my new love because he was a whole man. It didn't take much convincing on her part, he already felt like half a man with a limb missing."

"Why would she do that?" Rose with shaking hands put her cup down on the table. "Why?"

"Because your mother wanted Wilson. She always did. When he chose me over her she was livid. Why would he choose a plain woman over a beautiful woman like your mother?"

Odelia took another sip of coffee and wiped her mouth.

"Ruby went to see Wilson every day while he was in the hospital. Without his knowledge, she marked every letter I sent to him *return to sender,* unopened. When he was released, she helped him get an apartment close to the hospital so he could go to physical therapy. One night he asked her if he had gotten any mail from me, and she lied and told him no. That night he got drunk and they slept together. When he woke the next morning and remembered what he did, he asked her to leave."

Odelia sighed.

"Ruby was so angry with him. He admitted he had made a terrible mistake and that he still loved me and would always love only me. She left cursing him and that was the last he had any contact with our family until you showed up at his house."

Rose had never been so angry with anyone in her life, her mother had stooped to a new low. What a selfish woman that only cared for herself. She wrapped her arms around her waist to try to still her insides as they shook uncontrollable.

"I'm so sorry. I knew mother was spiteful but never did I believe her so heartless to do this to her own sister."

"Oh baby, none of this is your fault. No one carries the fault of her relatives. Your mother must carry all that blame. But there is more. That was the time when your mother met and married who you thought to be your father. After Wilson met you, he put two and two together and thought there was a very strong possibility that he was your father."

Rose inhaled and held her breath. "It can't be. She wouldn't have kept this from us. Would she?"

Aunt Odelia took Rose's hand in hers. "Wilson went to see your mother and made her confess the truth. You see, she thought she'd won. In her own wicked way, she thought she had something of Wilson I would never have, you.

But I love you like I could never have loved another child of my own blood."

"I have a father. Wilson is my dad. All these years when I needed one so badly, she knew, and all she did was make him dead in my eyes. Aunt Odelia I needed him. I needed him so much."

"Well you have him now, honey. He can't wait to do whatever it takes to make things up to you. I know you have been through so much. More than any child should have been through but it's not too late. It's not too late to share your life with a family."

Odelia drew in a breath and let it out slowly. "So, here's our plea to you. I know that all you want to do right now is run. Run as far away from Sam as you can. But think about this, you and your dad deserve a chance to get to know each other, a chance to make up a lifetime. Wilson and I are planning to get married in a week and want you to stand up for me."

Rose jumped up and started to pace. "I can't Aunt Odelia. I can't bear the thought of seeing Sam with Lisa and feeling the hurt I feel." Rose shuddered. "I know that they are a family and I'm the outsider. But to live under the same roof, sit at the same table, sleep in the room next to theirs? I can't." In a whisper, she added, "Please don't ask me."

"Rose we would never ask you to do something to add to your hurt. But the side house is finished and it is large enough for the three of us to live in. It has two bedrooms downstairs and an attic that has been made into a large suite. I had them finish that room, hoping you would stay, the day you showed up here. You never have to come into the big house again. Besides, where would you go, Rose? You have a family now. People that love you. Give us at least a week, until my wedding. I can have the boys move your stuff over to the suite now if you agree."

Rose pacing came to a halt at the window overlooking the galley. The place of the late night visits with Sam. A place of stolen kisses and hopeful promises. She had to get away. But as her aunt pointed out, where?

"Rose. Are you okay?"

"Sorry, Aunt Odelia, I was just thinking. I do so want to be here for your wedding. You and Wilson deserve happiness more than any couple I know." Rose turned away from the window and smiled at her aunt. "And I certainly can't go to Atlanta. Right now, I don't care if I ever see my mother again."

So enough about me, let's see about moving into the side house and planning a wedding. Besides it's not every day a girl gets to stand up for the bride in her dad's wedding."

"Honey child, thank you. And you'll see this is a good decision. We can help each other and be a family at the same time."

Sam dreaded breakfast with the family. Lisa had slept in one of the bedrooms near the girls. He did not want anyone thinking things were what they once were. Sam was not sure they ever could be. A lot of time and hurt had passed between them.

And then there was Rose. She was on his mind all night, and when he finally dozed off, she was in his dreams. He thought with Rose he had found his companion, his confidante, his lover. All the things he never had with Lisa.

He had to stop comparing the two of them. They were completely different. One the mother of his children, the other could have been the love of his life. He had to concentrate on what was best for Lizzy and Bea. If he wasn't careful, he could lose them and he knew his heart would stop.

Aw the hell with it, he would skip breakfast this morning or maybe drive into town to the new Tea Room. That way he wouldn't have to face any one.

Closing the door to his bedroom, he stopped in front of Rose's room. The door was ajar. He tapped on it.

"Rose, are you all right?" No answer.

Edging the door open, he surveyed the empty room. All of her stuff was gone. Sam entered the room and closed the door behind him. Her smell still lingered in the air. Gone, everything gone. He could expect nothing else. He had not given her a reason to stay.

Just as he turned to leave, the sunlight caught something bright in the fireplace. Sam bent and picked up the piece of broken snow globe in his hand. Turning it over he murmured, "I understand *bebé*. I don't believe in happy endings anymore, either."

Sam headed to the dining room. He knew he couldn't leave Bea and Lizzy to deal with their mother alone.

"Sit by me Papa, sit by me," Lizzy yelled the minute she saw him.

Lizzy and Bea sat on either side of him, as close as they could pull their chairs. Lisa was the only other person at the table. She sat across from them. A nervous smile on her lips.

"Good morning, Sam. You get up a lot later now. I remember you used to get up with the hens."

Lizzy giggled. Bea huffed. "He gets up with the chickens, not hens." Bea was not ready to forgive and forget.

"I'm sorry it's been awhile since I lived the country life."

Sam had to give credit where credit was due. Lisa was trying.

"Did you sleep well, Lisa?" Sam asked.

"Probably better than you did. Do you have plans for the day or can we all do something? You know, kind of get reacquainted."

Sam's hand froze, his fork in midair. He quickly looked at Bea and Lizzy, who in turn looked at him. Pleading. Bea was shaking her head no.

Had Lisa changed? She claimed to have. Could he trust her? These were her daughters too. Maybe he would let her prove herself to the girls.

"Let me get some chores done and we could go on a picnic."

"No! No picnic." Lizzy's lip began to quiver. "That is Miss Rose job, she takes us on picnics."

"Pumpkin, don't be rude. Your momma just wants to spend some time with you."

"It's okay, Sam. Time is what we all need. I've been gone for so long."

Lisa pasted on a smile and reached for Lizzy across the table.

Lizzy snatched her doll and ran toward the stairs.

"You shouldn't have come back, you know. Things were just fine without you." Bea spat and ran after Lizzy.

"Bea, come back here," Sam called after her.

"Let her go. I deserve this and more. Give them some time. But maybe you and I can still go." She touched his hand softly.

Sam couldn't help his reaction. He pulled his hand back and pretended to reach for another biscuit. "You can't expect to walk back into our lives and everyone take up where we left off. People change Lisa, feelings change." Sam stopped himself. He had to try, but not today. He took the biscuit and stood, I have to get some work done."

"Okay. But we really need to see if this is going to work. Or has Rose won your heart like she has won my daughters?"

"Don't go there, Lisa. Rose is gone and what she did or didn't do is none of your business." Sam surprised himself with his need to defend Rose. His arms still ached to hold her. Rose was a dream, Lisa a reality. She was still his wife and the mother of Lizzy and Bea. He had to do what was best from them.

"I'll come find you when I get through. Take it easy on the girls. They need to get to know you again. You broke their hearts you know."

Sam watched as Lisa processed his words and with a weak sigh walked to the doorway.

"I'll be in my room, let me know when you are ready."

Her thin tall body swayed as she walked, her head held high. Lisa always carried herself like a regal princess. She didn't look much older than the homecoming queen he once knew.

It had seemed perfectly natural when she came back to Bon Amie after a relationship gone wrong, carrying a small child, that he step up and make things right. He meant to give support, but she needed more and he wanted a family. He thought love would follow. But when she left after they had been married just barely a few years, she was gone for six months. Still he took her back. For Bea's sake. He loved that small girl and someone had to be a constant in her young life.

Love never followed. He knew that as he watched her walk upstairs. Not real love. Not the love he felt—. Damn, he had to get Rose out of his head. Concentrate on his children.

Sam found both of the girls in Bea's room. Bea as always was trying to comfort Lizzy. He closed the door behind him and sat on Bea's bed.

"Why don't we have a talk? You can ask me any questions and I'll give you as honest an answer as I can."

Bea cocked her head to one side. "We can ask you any question? Anything we want?"

"Yes, anything you want."

"Is she going to stay?" Bea asked.

Sam gazed down and saw the same look he had seen so many times in her young face. Rejection. Rejection came first by her biological dad and then by her mother on more than one occasion. So many people she gave her love to walked away.

"I don't know darlin'. She wants to. You remember what I told you when your mother left the first time?"

"Yes. You said she left, not because she wanted to leave us, but because she couldn't stay. But you never told us why she couldn't stay." Bea twisted the tail of a stuffed animal she'd picked up from her bed. "So after she never called or came to see us, I figured she just didn't love us enough."

Sam fought the lump in his throat. What people do to their children. "Bea why didn't you come and talk to me about this? You knew I would always tell you the truth. You're wrong, darlin', your mother loves you too much. She left because some grown-ups can't live in a place where they feel confined. They need a place to fly and be free, and your mom is one of those grown-ups. But most of all she needs the two of you to love her back."

"Papa, I have a question." Lizzy's small sweet voice melted his heart.

"What's that, pumpkin?" Sam managed to say.

"What about Miss Rose? Do we have to stop loving her now?"

From the mouth of babies. "No pumpkin, you can love Miss Rose as long as you live. I know she will always love you. I'm sorry you didn't get to say goodbye to her, she must have left last night."

"Miss Rose didn't leave, Dad. She moved in with Odelia in the side house early this morning. She said we could go see her anytime if it was okay with you and our her," Bea chimed in.

Sam's heart gave a lunge. Rose was still here. Did that news make him happy or not? It sure complicated things.

"How long is she staying? Never mind we were talking about your mom."

"It's okay, Papa, you said we could talk about anything. Miss Rose is staying for Odelia's wedding. I get to throw flowers and Bea gets to stand somewhere with Odelia and Miss Rose."

"Odelia is getting married? Did I miss a whole day somewhere? How do you two know so much?"

"Because we listen, don't we Bea?"

Sam couldn't help but smile as Bea's face turned a light pink. "Bea, have you been eavesdropping? You know that is not something we do?"

"Yes, Dad. But sometimes that's the only way we find out anything."

"This discussion is not over, Bea. And to think you have pulled your little sister into this bad habit with you."

Sam hissed air through his lips. He knew he was overreacting, but his mind would not let go of the knowledge that Rose was still nearby.

CHAPTER FIFTEEN

Rose excitement grew as her Aunt twirled around in the dress they had found. The soft cream color set off Odelia's olive complexion. Her smile was infectious, her happiness contagious.

"Mercy, to think that in three days I'll be Mrs. Wilson James. Oh, how I've waited for this day."

"Yes you have, and no one deserves happiness more than you, Aunt Odelia. This has been a long time coming, but you never gave up hope." Rose smiled at her sweet aunt. "You look like a girl twenty years old. Wilson is a very luck man."

Laughing, Odelia took Rose's hands in hers and spun her around with her. "Honey child, it is me that is lucky. I found my Wilson and I know you will always be a part of my life too."

Stopping before a full-length mirror she studied herself. "Do you think I need a hat or a veil? A hat, definitely a hat."

They finished the shopping and stopped at the café for lunch. Mildred, the waitress, a woman about Odelia's age sat them by the window.

"Well, well, what's this I hear about you getting married? You sure have breathed air into us old maids. Maybe we have a chance after all. Good for you I say, good for you. Now what can I get you two to eat?"

Rose caught a glimpse of a gold tooth in the front of Mildred's mouth as she smiled; it sat next to a missing one dead center. Her skin was smooth with no wrinkles and her head was topped off with a full set of curls in a light purple.

"What a delightful woman. Has she been a friend of yours long?" Rose asked.

"Since we were little girls. Her love was killed in the war like I was afraid my Wilson had been."

A tap on the window turned both of their heads. There stood Bea, Lizzy, Sam and Lisa. Rose thought her heart had stopped. It was the first time she had seen Sam since the night of the dance. She couldn't help her eyes from locking on his. Lizzy was asking him a question and the two girls ran inside leaving Sam and Lisa still on the outside.

Sam's jaw was tense and tight, his eyes full of turmoil. He tried a weak smile but his lips resisted. Lisa took his arm and led him away from the window, across the street to a bench in the park.

Rose took a breath. She realized she had been holding it since they tapped on the window.

"Hi, Miss Rose. Odelia, did you find a wedding dress?" Bea asked.

Rose concentrated on the girls and told them in detail about the wedding dress and hat.

"Have you two eaten lunch?" Rose asked.

"Yeah, we ate with Papa and—" Lizzy stopped and looked at Rose.

"It's okay, Lizzy, you can talk about your mom. What did you eat?"

"Hot dogs. Mom said that was her favorite when she was a little girl. Do you believe she was ever a little girl?"

"All ladies were once little girls. I bet she was a pretty one, don't you?" Rose tried to keep herself as calm as she could for Bea and Lizzy's sake. They deserved a mom and a dad. "She sure is beautiful now, don't you agree?" Rose said.

Lizzy turned her head to the side as if in thought and put her arm around Rose's neck and ran her little fingers through Rose's curls.

"Yeah, she's beautiful. Just like the dolls that come in red boxes tied with gold bows."

Bea never spoke, but watched Rose and Lizzy from hooded eyebrows. "We better go Lizzy, Dad said we could only visit a little while."

Before they walked away from the table, Bea turned around and ran back to Rose. "I know she hurt you, too. I'm sorry. But I'll always love you Rose. Dad said we have to give her a chance," she whispered.

Rose heart ached for the two girls she had grown to love so much joined the couple on the bench. Lisa held Lizzy's hand and reached for Bea's, but the little girl held it close to her body. As they walked away, Sam looked back and Rose ducked her head. She could not allow him to peer into her heart again. A hand covered hers just as their lunch arrived. She looked at Aunt Odelia through glazed eyes.

"I'm so sorry Rose. This is very hard on you. You're not staying are you?"

"I can't," Rose whispered. "If I do I'll lose myself. I have to find a place for me."

"Where? Do you know?"

"Maybe, I contacted a fellow writer friend of mine that lives in the mountains of Colorado. A friend of hers has a cabin not far from her home and said that the area is great for writing. So I sent her money to secure the cabin. It has two bedrooms so you and Wilson can visit. I don't want to lose touch with my family now that I have one, as small as it is." Rose mustered up a smile. "I already love Wilson and am enjoying the fact that he's my dad."

"I wish things could be different. I am going to miss seeing you every day. Now eat. You have picked at that food, and I don't believe you have eaten a bite, and I'm afraid you will waste away."

"I'm really not hungry. If you are through, why don't we stop by Trudy's and see if she is finished with your bridal bouquet? I told Bea and Lizzy we would practice walking down the aisle this afternoon, and I would like to wrap their gifts for them before they get there."

Trudy was working on a casket cover when they walked in and she flashed them a grin.

"Well if it's not the bride. Came to see what a mess I made?" She tucked in a lone carnation and went into her cooler. Trudy returned with a nosegay of pale pink roses surrounding a beautiful magnolia. Pink and cream ribbons were tied with a pretty bow and streamed down together like a waterfall.

"Trudy, it's absolutely beautiful. I couldn't be happier." Odelia dabbed at her eyes. "If the two of you will excuse me a moment, something's in my eye."

"I agree. You are a master at what you do, Trudy. The colors are great the flowers will accent her dress perfectly. It is so good to see her so happy, don't you agree?"

"Yes, but I am more concerned with the lack of happiness in my good friend. How are you?"

"Getting by, Trudy, just getting by."

"Are you up to a girl party tomorrow night? We could share a beer or two and maybe a pot of fudge," Trudy teased.

"You know that might be what I need. Minus the fudge, the memory of the last time I did that is still too fresh in my mind. Why don't you come over to Aunt Odelia's? This can be her bachelorette party. If you don't mind getting in touch with Susan, I have something to do with the girls.."

"No problem. Let's keep it a surprise. What about Bea and Lizzy?" Trudy was getting into the swing of planning a party now.

"I'll tell them this afternoon. But we'll need to save the beer for when they go to bed. I've already bought Aunt Odelia a pretty nightgown. This will be so good for me to focus on her. She is everything to me. Anyone else you can think of we need to invite? I don't want it to be too big." Rose said.

"Lisa?" asked Trudy.

"Hell no." Rose grinned. "Did I say that out loud? I'm sorry but she has everything she wanted, and besides this is about my aunt and she bares no bones about the way she feels about Lisa."

"Don't be too sure, Rose. She might not have everything she wants, it looks that way now, but don't be too sure." Trudy winked at Rose.

Susan brought Odelia a beautiful pink robe and matching slippers. Trudy's box held a naughty black number. Bea and Lizzy, Rose's help, made her a book of wishes. The party was off to a good start.

"Hey, may I have your attention?" Rose raised her glass of apple cider to propose a toast. "I wanted to say how happy I am that I came here this summer. I'm sorry it took so long to get to know this wonderful woman. She is much more to me than an aunt, she is the mother I never had, and to make life better she gave me the dad I thought was dead."

Rose took her time dwelling on the other two women and the two little girls. "I think of all of you as family and cherish each and every one of you. May happiness follow you, Aunt Odelia, every day of the year."

The room became quite, each woman in her own thoughts.

Trudy cleared her throat and raised her glass. "Rose is right, you need happiness, but most of all you are going to need luck, Odelia. The older these boys get the more you need luck to keep them in line. You just need to look in their eyes and see the mischief in them. Big ole brown eyes full of fun. Except Sam, what color are his anyway?"

"You know I can't put a real color to Sam's eyes, they sort of change," said Odelia.

"They are light blue with streaks of green in them when he is excited." Rose looked down at her folded hands, closed her eyes and continued. "When he's frustrated, they turn a darker blue green with a circle of brown. And when he talks to his family with pride and love in his voice, they turn a soft gray with amber sparks. That's what color Sam's eyes are."

Odelia broke the silence as everyone seemed to be holding their breath. "Thank you, Rose," she blew her nose. "Thank all of you for a great party, but a bride needs her beauty rest, so if the rest of you will excuse me, I'll take this tired body and two tired little girls, and we will say our good nights."

Susan excused herself also stating she needed to get back to the baby, who was still on breast milk. Trudy and Rose began picking up.

"Okay girlfriend, it's time for a beer and real talk. Tell me how are you really doing?" Trudy asked.

Rose kicked off her shoes and sat on the love seat tucking her feet under her. She took a long sip of the beer and motioned for Trudy to sit beside her.

"Numb. I think I'm numb. The other night at the dance was a nightmare.

I don't think I've ever been that hurt. Not even when old Ted dumped me at the altar. Not when all the other men pushed me away. Not even when my so called mother degraded me." Rose took another drink and set the bottle on the small table in front of them. "I know now it's because none of them meant as much to me as he does." Rose laughed. "Listen to me, I can't even say his name."

"Oh, Rose, I wish— "

"It's okay. I don't regret coming. I have so much more than I did when I came, for one thing a friendship with you. But I have a favor to ask? The cabin in Colorado wont be ready for awhile and I think the two newlyweds will need the house to themselves. Besides I hate to leave the man that I now call dad until we've had more time to get to know each other." Laughter flowed from Rose. "Oh yeah, the favor. The short of it is I need a place to stay until the cabin is ready."

Trudy stood and grabbed hold of Rose's hands. Do you mean you are willing to stay a while longer?"

"Yes but not so near Sam's home. Do you know of a place, maybe in town?

"Do I know of a place? You bet I do, if you don't mind small. Remember that little garage apartment out back? I just finished painting it. I would love to have you there." Trudy took a breath. "I think you could find a place to set up a writing station. You haven't given up writing have you?"

"No. I could never give up writing. But I might try my hand at another genre. Time will tell about that. You know, the one thing Aunt Odelia taught me to believe in was happy endings. I know now they do happen. Just not to everyone."

"Are you sure? About the apartment, I'll pay rent of course and that is not negotiable."

"Great. Who knows you might like living in town so much you will forget about Colorado. Well, it's late and we both need our beauty sleep. But you know I'm just a phone call away; please call me anytime of the night or day. Even if you just need to talk. I love you and I'm going to miss you more than you know. Try to get some sleep. You're too young to be toting such big bags under your eyes."

Trudy was right. She did need to sleep, but that was easier said than done.

Rose pulled back the curtains and gazed at the big house. She could see the gallery and Sam's door; the lights in his bedroom were still on. Was Lisa with him? Was she in his arms? Were they making love? What was wrong with her? *The sooner I get away from here the better.*

Rose lifted her head and brushed the back of her hand across her eyes. She gave a last look at the big house and noticed that this time Sam's door was open. The light from his bedroom highlighted the lone figure on the gallery. Sam. He wore only pants and no shirt. How much did she recognize that look? Their late night visits on the gallery, he dressed the same. She could still feel the warmth and tautness of his chest as she placed her hands on the windowpane.

Rose tore her gaze to his face that was turned in her direction. Was he looking at her? Did he know how much she was longing for him? The distance made it difficult to see his expression but his body language told her of his sadness.

"Two lost souls, Sam. We are two lost souls, you and I. We wanted something that could never be." She pulled the curtain close. It was turning into the longest week of her life.

CHAPTER SIXTEEN

The day of the wedding was hectic. Odelia and Wilson had decided to hold the ceremony on the road leading to the *Annees Passees* under the canopy of the oak trees. Trudy was putting the last touches to Rose's hair, a wreath of tiny cream-colored rose buds, when the door swung open.

Lizzy and Bea fretted with their beautiful dresses. Bea pulled at the neck and tugged at the large bow covering her waist. Lisa had insisted on dressing them, including doing their hair. She'd piled it up on their head making them both look years older. A tinge of pink rouge and pink lipstick adorned their face. Lizzy's hair had started to slip and she was trying to shove it back straight.

"Oh, Miss Rose, you look like a princess. Do we look like princesses, too?" Lizzy asked.

"You sure do. You both look good enough to eat." That was met with a squeal of delight.

Rose bent down and hugged Lizzy and Bea. "You know, the other night at the party, I had a gift for each of you but forgot to give it to you. Do you want to open them now?"

"I guess. It's because you are leaving after the wedding, right?" Bea asked. Her small shoulders slumped in sadness.

"That's right, Bea. I am leaving, but I'm going to move into town for awhile until my place is ready in Colorado. So we are not going to goodbye, okay?"

"Okay. But you don't have to leave. She won't bother you. She stays to herself most of the time anyway. But dad says she's trying," Bea replied.

"Sit here on the floor and I'll get your gifts."

The girls each got one gift and there was a big box attached to both of them. Bea opened hers first and pulled a big purple journal with a purple feather pen out of the box. With it was a book on storytelling and a set of leather bound books to read. *The Little Women* series.

Bea put her arms around Rose's neck and hugged her very tight. "Thank you, Rose," she whispered.

Lizzy tore open her box and pulled out another rag doll, this one with red curly hair and big blue eyes.

"I thought Abby needed a friend. Because since I met you two, I know how important friends are. You and Abby can give her a name."

"She already has a name." Lizzy said, looking adoringly at her new doll. "Her name is Rosie, and I will love her always."

The small girl threw herself into Rose's arms and hugged like she would never let go.

"Open the other box, girls," Trudy said.

They worked on the box together and lifted a lap desk for each of them, filled with stamped post cards addressed to Rose at her new address.

"Now neither of you will have any excuse not to write to me and keep me in touch with what the two of you are up to. When I move to Colorado. We better get going, I don't want Aunt Odelia to think we all forgot her wedding."

The music started and Rose walked up the aisle escorted by Lewis. Everyone was standing. Sam stood next to Lisa, her hand resting on his arm. A notice, Rose thought, letting everyone know "he's mine, this one is taken."

Her eyes met Sam's and for a moment she forgot to breathe. She had not seen him since the night of the dance except from a distance. He looked tired. He looked good. His eyes sucking her in like they always did. Rose stumbled and he reached out to her but Lewis caught her, and she tore her gaze from Sam. It will be over soon.

The wedding march sounded and Lizzy entered, throwing magnolia petals on the ground. Her hair looked a mess. Half was down, the other half slipping. She had wiped her lips and smeared the lipstick down her chin, but all and all she still looked like an angel.

Rose stole a look at Lisa and saw the look of horror that consumed her. Sam was in awe, the look of love and amusement all over his face.

Aunt Odelia entered next, escorted by her Wilson and Bea behind her. Bea was trying so hard to be grown up. She carried herself tall and took big steps as she tried to walk like a grown woman, which made her sway a little too much. She looked like a little girl in a body working too hard to be an adult. .

"Who gives this woman to wed this man?" the preacher asked.

"I do," answered Rose.

The vows went smoothly, and Rose never thought her aunt looked more beautiful or happier. Wilson, her dad, stood tall and was dressed in his uniform. He said he made Odelia a promise he would return after the war; his war took a little longer. They were pronounced man and wife and he kissed her gently. They would now live their happier ever after, this Rose had no doubt.

Rose hugged and kissed all the brothers, Susan, Trudy, Bea, and Lizzy. She lingered over Aunt Odelia and Wilson. "Promise me the two of you will come to town often," she said.

"Nothing could keep us away. Besides I owe my bride a break from cooking once a week or more. And I've got my favorite daughter to see." Wilson hugged her tight and kissed her cheek.

Rose walked to her car she had packed that morning. She ran up the steps of the side house to get her purse and take one last look at the world she wished she could have.

"Were you going to drive away without telling me goodbye?"

The sound of Sam's voice shook her to her core.

He was leaning against the door of her car. His easy stance much as it was when she first came, except now the look on his face was different. His eyes still held hers, seeking, pleading, always wanting something she couldn't give.

"I thought we had said our goodbyes that night, Sam. I don't think we have anything else to say to one another. I do give my thanks to you for opening your home to me that night. I needed a place to regroup. And thank you for allowing the girls to visit me when I get to Colorado sometimes. I really am going to miss them."

She stood in front of him now. He had not moved.

"Do you know how much I care for you, Rose?" he whispered. "How much I wished things could be different, how much I regret being the cause of such pain. I hated Ted for what he did to you. Admired you that you could start new. But now I'm no better than he was and you are the one left holding the hurt. You are the one that has to start new once again. If I could go back. If—"

"You can't, Sam. None of us can. Take care of yourself. Take care of your family."

He put his hand on her arm, but she pulled away. "Please don't. I can't take anymore. Please move. Walk away. Let me go, Sam, let me go."

He moved out of the way, and she got in the car and started the motor. He stood glaring at her.

"You were right. That first night I came. A redheaded woman on a Monday brought you nothing but trouble." Rose gunned the motor and drove away.

Sam watched as the dust settled on the winding road leading from the plantation. "You're wrong, Rose. You brought me a lot more than trouble."

"You let her go. I thought you had more sense than that, little brother."

Sam whirled around to see Preston standing behind him. "I did what I had to do. Don't you start with me. I did what I had to do."

"Really, for who? Ask yourself that question. For who?"

Sam clenched his fist. I told you not to mess with me. Now walk away."

"Why, so you can feel proud that you sacrificed your feelings for everyone else again? The martyr suit doesn't fit you this time, Sam."

"You don't know what the hell you are talking about. I never set out to me a martyr."

"Maybe that's the wrong choice of words. But think about it. You gave up Little League so you could stay home with the twins when Mom died. You gave up your scholarship so you could run the farm when Dad got sick. You gave up your freedom when Lisa came back to town with a small child. Every day, you give up parts of yourself to help this family. Time has come, my brother. Time to do something that's for your good. Not the good of the family."

They stood facing each other, neither spoke; they both had said all they could say. Preston shook his head and walked away.

He's crazy. No one knew. He had responsibilities. Everyone couldn't just throw responsibilities to the wind to make himself happy.

Sam's thoughts turned to Rose, like they did almost every second of the day. Emptiness filled his soul. How was he to make it through a day without knowing she was here?

"Look, Papa. Look what Miss Rose gave me. Her name is Rosie, 'cause she looks like Miss Rose and she is soft and full of love like Miss Rose. Don't you like her, Papa? I think she's the most beautiful doll I've ever seen. Except Abby. They are going to be best friends, just like me and Miss Rose, don't you agree?"

"Yes pumpkin, I agree. I'm glad Miss Rose gave you something to remember her by. That was very kind of her."

"Did she give you a gift to remember her by, Papa?"

"Yes she did, pumpkin. But what she gave me I will keep inside here." He pointed to his chest. "And I will always remember Rose."

"I miss her already, Papa."

"I do too, pumpkin, I do too. Let's go see what your mother and Bea are doing?"

"Mommy is lying down. She said the wedding was too stressful. I think she was upset about my hair falling down. I tried to push it up but it wouldn't stay."

"I thought you were one of the prettiest girls there, pumpkin. Your mom didn't yell at you, did she?

"No, Papa. She is always smiling. Kind of a funny smile. Can you frown and smile at the same time, Papa?"

Laughing, Sam picked up Lizzy and carried her back to the house. He knew exactly the look on Lisa's face Lizzy was describing. A forced smile that hid her frustration. She was trying too hard. He would let her rest and then check on her later.

Odelia left plenty of food prepared in the fridge. Preston and the twins were busy heating up a taste of everything. Lewis had gone home with Susan and Penny. Odelia and Wilson went to their house. All would be back to normal soon.

Sam fixed himself and the girls each a plate and they sat at the table. Talking was strained. Sam knew his brothers were upset with him for letting Rose go. He shoved a fork of food in his mouth, but it stuck in his throat like bad medicine. Sam had to make things as normal as he could for the sake of the girls.

In time everyone would forget about Rose. But would he?

Rose settled into the small apartment and smiled at the fresh flowers Trudy had placed on the table. She'd also managed to round up a small desk with a lamp and a comfy chair. She knew the sooner Rose could get back to work the better.

A routine soon developed with Trudy and Rose sharing coffee in the morning on Trudy's patio. The rest of the day Rose spent walking around Bon Amie, and visiting with the people. Sometimes she made notes about one character trait or another of the friendly people. Her favorite time was when

Odelia and Wilson came and they shared stories, mostly about her dad's life and sometimes hers. She even found happiness hearing about the LeBlanc brothers and of course Bea and Lizzy. Because she would be going to Colorado soon a decision was made she would not try to see Bea or Lizzy, another goodbye for them would be too hard.

As Rose sat at her desk trying desperately to finds words to make a story on the page she realized she had to end another part of her life before she started new. She had to confront her mother.

The travel plans were set and as she flew away from the support of her dad and aunt she knew she would always be loved and that was a new beginning.

When her mother answered the door she also knew this would be the last time she would enter this house.

"Well, what have you done this time, Rose? Did you run out of welcome or money?"

Her mother sat in a stiff white brocade chair, and arranged her silk caftan around her feet, such a difference from the small green chair that use to sit by her aunts window.

Rose refused to sit. "I know this will surprise you mother, but neither my lack of welcome or money has brought me here today. I came to tell you that you don't own me anymore." Rose held her hand up to shush her mother and continued. "You see I don't need to jump through hoops to please my real parent, my dad. He loves me no matter what. Oh and did you know he and Aunt Odelia are happily married now? So I just wanted you to know you don't have to worry about me anymore, in fact you don't have to think about me anymore. I now have a family. Without you." Rose closed the door behind her and let the sadness lift from her shoulders.

"Well, Rose, this is your new start. Make the most of it. You are a strong woman and you don't need the woman that gave you life, and neither do you need a man. In time, you'll even forget about Sam." Under her breath she whispered, "Yeah right, if you live.

CHAPTER SEVENTEEN

Two weeks had passed since Rose left. Odelia and Wilson made every excuse to go into town. The second planting would start soon. Lisa and Bea and Lizzy were getting by. Everyone was struggling to return to some kind of normalcy.

Sam sat on the gallery next to Rose's empty room. He still couldn't share his room with Lisa. His arms still ached for Rose, and his heart still beat for her. It wouldn't be fair to Lisa. He replayed all the times he and Rose had sat on this same gallery talking late into the night.

His family use to share a lot of laughter, but he hadn't heard that sound in weeks. A dark cloud hung over *Annees Passee*.

Words that Preston spoke to him the day of the wedding still pulled at his mind. Was he making a mistake? Could he live the rest of his life a shell of a man?

He heard a soft knock on his door. "Come in, it's open."

Lisa walked in and was headed for the gallery, but Sam hurried inside. He couldn't share that spot with Lisa either.

"Is everything all right, Lisa?"

"Fine, everything is fine. How about you, Sam, are you fine?"

Sam took a deep breath and knew what he had to do. For this one time he had to do something for him.

"No, I'm not. Please sit, we need to talk."

Lisa sat in the chair near the bed and he sat on his bed but immediately got up and started pacing.

"Lisa, this is not going to work."

"Sam, I—."

"Wait let me finish, please. I've tried Lisa, but I can't live a lie this time. We made a mistake once, we can't make it again." He stopped pacing and stared at Lisa's perfect face, but what he longed for was a tiny mole just at the top of a lip. And a lots of red curls bouncing around that face. He needed Rose's face.

"I'm in love with Rose, and if she can't be in my life I don't know what I'll do. She makes me feel whole, Lisa. I'm sorry. I don't want to hurt you, but I can't go on like this. I need Rose. Do you understand?"

"Yes. I understand. I don't love you either. I don't think either one of us was ever in love with the other. We tried to make our lives into something we thought we both needed. I don't belong here, Sam. I never was cut out to be a farmer's wife. I'm not really cut out to be a full-time mother. I love the girls, but we don't connect. You know." Her face became animated. "I belong in the city. New York is my home. I need the noise, the action, and the excitement. Have I messed everything up by coming back?"

Sam was on his knees in front of Lisa, holding her hands in his. "No, I think we both have been given a second chance. We will sit down and decide how we will share the girls and let them know how much we both love them and will never desert them. Tomorrow, we will see a lawyer about a divorce, is that too soon for you?"

"Oh no, Sam. If I could be back in New York next week, I could save my lease on my loft. I was so afraid you wouldn't let me see the girls if I ran away again, but I dying here. I want to show them New York. Take them to plays, to the museums, shopping. This will work, I know it will." Lisa bent over and kissed Sam on the cheek.

"I have a thousand things to do. I need to call my friends tonight. Thank you, Sam. And if truth be known, Rose is getting one heck of a man."

"If she'll have me."

"Are you kidding, she has farmer's wife written all over her." Lisa laughed and floated out the room.

Sam let out the breath he thought he had been holding since Rose left. "Wait for me, Rose. I'm coming."

Sam came to the table the next morning whistling. For the first time in a long time, he felt completely free. The sun would shine today.

"What's gotten into you?" Preston asked.

"Nothing. Can't a man whistle if he wants?

Lizzy and Bea watchful eyes watched as the brothers teased each other.

Odelia came in from the kitchen carrying a plate full of biscuits. "What's going on in here? Did I hear someone laugh? I thought we had all given that up."

"Papa's happy," Lizzy said.

"Oh, did something happen?" Ellie asked.

"I have nothing to tell yet. Girls, your mom and I want to talk to you this afternoon, so don't wander off. Lisa and I are going to town this morning, see you all later." Sam planted a kiss on Lizzy's head and on Bea's then plopped one on Odelia's cheek.

Odelia and Preston looked at each other. Unspoken words passed between them.

"Let's go see the new calf. Wilson said he was going to wash her off today." Bea pulled Lizzy away from the table and they rushed outside.

Lisa and Sam bounced down the stairs and yelled their goodbyes.

"I don't like it, Preston. Something is not right. You don't suppose the two of them have made up do you?"

"No way. Do you think?"

"Well something happened."

"Maybe he called Rose," Preston offered.

"No. I talked to her this morning. She's putting up a good front, but the sadness is still in her voice." Odelia puckered her lips and let out a held breath.

"I don't understand why love has to hurt so much."

"It won't hurt me, Sweet Odelia," Preston teased.

"Well, Preston LeBlanc. Do you have something to tell me?"

"Not yet. I'm still working on something. I have to tell the others that we need to get our work done early so we can be here when the bomb hits."

Sam and Lisa made easy decisions and chatted like old friends on their way back to the plantation. "I want the girls to be all right about this. I can't handle them being sad again."

"They won't, Sam. Maybe this time they will have a mother that will be able to feel comfortable in her own skin and not so awkward with them. And they always have you and maybe Rose."

"What about you, Lisa? Do you have someone?"

"Maybe. I just started seeing someone before I left. He's a producer, and I think he is someone that I could really be interested in. He has the loft next to mine. We'll see."

Bea and Lizzy looked so scared when Sam and Lisa sat down in front of them.

"Okay, as always you can ask us any questions you want when we are through with our news. The very most important thing you both need to know is that we both love you very much," Sam said, reaching out and taking their hands in his.

"I have told both of you these past weeks that I moved to New York City when I left here. And I was very happy there, but I had a hole in my heart. That hole was the two of you. I missed you like crazy. But sometimes people can't live in the country. Do you understand?"

"Like the country mouse and the city mouse. You're the city mouse and Papa's the country mouse, like us. Right Papa?" Lizzy said.

"Right pumpkin. But what—"

"So what you are saying is that you are leaving again, right?" Bea interrupted.

"That's right baby, but this time it's different. Your dad and I have made some plans. If they are all right with the two of you, you will live with your dad, but visit me in the city on arranged days and any other times you want. I'll take you to the theater and shopping and a thousand other places. We'll eat in fancy restaurants and walk on Broadway." Lisa's face was so excited that Lizzy got excited too.

"We can be both city and country mice." Lizzy squealed.

"But will you keep your promises. Will you really come and get us to go stay with you in New York? Or will this be another lie?" Bea said.

"Bea, watch what you say." Sam warned.

"It's all right, Sam. Bea has asked a very good question. No, baby, I will not break this promise. You see I wanted you, but was afraid if I asked your dad after the way I just left last time, he would say no to all visitations. I was wrong. Your dad is a very understanding man. And we plan to work very hard together making sure no promises are ever broken again."

Bea shrugged her shoulders. "It's okay then I guess. It might be kind of fun having two very different homes. And I've always wanted to see a Broadway show. When are you leaving?"

"In a couple of days. But we will see each other at Thanksgiving. Your dad said he would fly you two up in time to see the Macy's Thanksgiving Parade. That will give me enough time to get your room ready. I do love you girls. Are we all okay?"

"Yes. We're okay, right Bea?"

"I think so. Will our room be next to yours?"

"Yes, Bea, right next to mine. We'll have fun you'll see. I need to place a call to arrange my flight, I'll see you at dinner."

"Any questions, girls?" Sam asked as he picked them both up and sat each of them on a knee.

Lizzy looked around the room and whispered. "What about Miss Rose? Papa, can she come back when mom is gone?"

"I don't know pumpkin. Maybe."

"Mom really love us now, dad?" Bea asked.

"Yes, darling, she really does. Now if neither of you have any other questions, then go wash up for dinner."

When the parlor door opened people scattered in all directions.

"Okay you guys, I know you were listing. Come ask your questions."

Preston, Rusty and Randy, Odelia and Wilson crept around the corner. Each with a sheepish look on their face.

"We didn't hear very much, just Lisa ranting about New York. What's going on?" Rusty spoke up.

The girls ran by giggling and Sam invited them all back into the parlor.

"Lisa and I filed for divorce this morning. It is a combined decision and a friendly one. We have also decided on visitation rights on her behalf. We both admitted we made a mistake, and we don't need to make another staying in a loveless marriage. So that is it in a nutshell. The girls are coping with the idea, and I think it is best for everyone. Everyone deserves to be happy including me."

Everyone was quiet, until Preston jumped up. "Hot damn, you're going after Little Rose aren't you? "

Sam grinned.

"Sam? Are you going after Rose?" Odelia asked with wishful plea in her eyes.

"I'm making plans. That's all I have to say."

"What about the planting, Sam? You can't wait that long, Rose will be headed for Colorado in two days."

"I got brothers that know this farm as well as I do. It's time they take on some of the responsibility. If they think they are up to the job."

"We can all out work you any day, brother, and don't you forget it," Preston said in fun. He shook Sam's hand and patted his back. "You've made me proud, Sam. Now bring her back to this family. Her family."

CHAPTER EIGHTEEN

Rose returned from the walk that she took every afternoon. The sun was about to set on another wasted day. So far, she had not been able to write one word, and her appetite had not returned. But it was the lack of sleep that still bothered her the most. She tossed all night and then slept in the wee hours of the morning only to wake still exhausted.

She opened the front door she never bothered to lock and put some water on the stove for tea. "What I wouldn't do for one of Aunt Odelia's cup of dark roast coffee about now." she said.

"Still talking to yourself, I see," Sam said coming from the loft.

"Gracious. Are you crazy? You scared me half to death." Rose clutched her chest. Was she scared are just so glad to see him? She didn't know.

"What are you doing here?"

"I came for this, *bebé*." With one swift move he held her in his arms and lowered his lips to hers. Pulling her as close as he could, holding on for dear life.

They held on to each other, their lips melting into one until they both had to come up for air.

"Stop, Sam. What are you doing? I can't do this."

"It's okay, my sweet, Rose. I choose you. Don't you see you are the only one it can be? You are the one I love."

Rose's legs gave out, maybe from the lack of food, exhaustion, or maybe from the hope she now felt. Sam caught her and carried her to the sofa.

"Lisa and I filed for a divorce and she has returned to New York. And I've come to bring you home, if you'll come. Please say you'll come."

Rose began to shake and Sam pulled her to him again. This is where she belonged, in Sam's arms. If he held her forever, it would not be long enough.

"Are you sure, Sam? Because if you're not I can't bear to say goodbye again."

"I'm sure, Rose. I have never been surer of anything in my life. You were the first girl I ever kissed and I want you to be the last girl I ever kiss."

Rose managed a smile, and then said through shaking lips, "I need to pack."

Sam kissed her slowly at first, making both of them groan. Allowing herself to let go, without fear of doing something wrong.

A low whistle sounded in the background. Releasing Rose, Sam looked around the room. "What is that noise?"

"The kettle!" Rose jumped off the bed and bounded over to the stove with Sam in pursuit. Turning off the stove, she turned and bumped into Sam.

"You didn't have to come with me."

"Yes I did. You are not getting out of my sight tonight. I don't want to ever let you go again. Now let's get that packing done. You have family waiting for you."

Rose cuddled up next to Sam's side, his arm folded around her in the most natural way.

Rose began to cry. All the built up wanting and sadness just erupted.

Sam took her in his arms. "Aw, *bebé* I know I hurt you."

He started to let her go but she held him so tight. "Sam I'm not crying because you hurt me, but because you loved me, life has been so good to me,

Sam. To find a man like you and to know that with you, I am enough." Rose snuggled next to Sam and they talked and made plans.

As Rose and Sam walked out of Trudy's front door they were holding hands. They almost ran right into the Mouton sisters who gave both of them a once over and Mavis even winked before they strolled off down the street.

"Well it looks like we will be front page news in the Mouton express today," Sam said. "Let's go home."

Sam turned the wheel and his truck drove onto the road leading to the plantation she let out a sigh.

"We're home. Are you happy?" Sam asked.

"You bet I am. Do you think everyone will be here? I can't wait to see the girls. You said they were all right about me coming back, right?"

"Are you kidding, they can't wait. They missed you, Rose, we all did. But I don't know if everyone will be here."

They pulled up in front of the house but no one came to meet them. Rose was disappointed.

Sam held the door open for her and she entered the house she had so grown to love that summer.

"Where is everyone? It's never this quiet?" Rose asked.

"Maybe they are in here." Sam led her into the parlor.

Rose gasped. In the middle of the room stood the biggest Christmas tree she had ever seen. All decked out with decorations and lights.

"Sam what is this?"

Sam turned on the lights in the room and everyone came out of hiding. Lizzy and Bea ran into Rose's arms. Her beloved Aunt Odelia stood in the arms of Rose's dad, Wilson. And all of the boys, Lewis, Preston, Rusty and Randy grinned through moist eyes. Susan and Penny walked in behind Trudy.

"Welcome home," They all said in unison.

"The tree was Preston and the girls' idea. They said you never had a Christmas tree or a real family and we all thought it was time you had both," Sam said as he handed her a box wrapped in red paper tied in a gold bow.

Rose sat on the sofa with the girls on either side. "Don't worry, it's not one of those pretty dolls," Lizzy said.

Rose opened the box and removed a snow globe with a family inside, all smiling, all in front of a big house.

"Look on the bottom." Sam said.

A ring was stuck to the bottom. Sam helped her remove it and got down on his knee in front of her.

"Rose, if you will have me, and all of them," he gestured to his family, "I will take a lifetime giving you your happy ever after."

Rose looked from one to the other of Sam's family, that had been her family of the heart all summer, and smiled.

"Sam, you have already given me my happy ever after. Yes, yes, yes."

Cheers erupted around the room. Aunt Odelia was in tears.

"Hey big brother, know what day it is? It's Monday," his brothers said together.

Sam picked Rose up in his arms and grinned a slow grin.

"Monday is my favorite day. You boys are going to have to find your own trouble. This one is mine."

About the Author

Award-winning author, Hattie Mae was born and bred southern, cutting her teeth on cornbread and greens and running barefoot through the canals of her small Louisiana town. So when it came to writing, there was no question as to where to set her books.

She's now writing her fourth book set in Bon Amie, a busy little town nestled in the heart of Cajun country. She's also published a short story in The Cup Of Comfort For Teachers. The love of books and writing runs in her family, Hattie's daughter is National Bestselling historical romance author, Robyn DeHart.

When not writing you can usually find her playing with her grandchildren or cooking up some healthy versions of tasty southern fare. She lives in central Texas with her husband and one crazy cat.

You can find Hattie on her website: http://www.hattiemaeauthor.com/

Look for more Bon Amie novels coming soon...